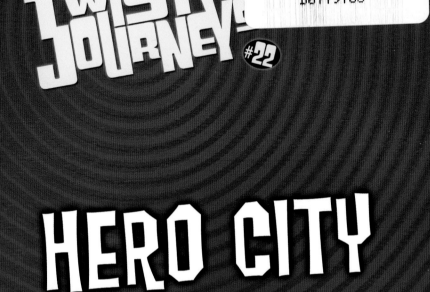

HERO CITY

Evonne Tsang & Adan Jimenez

illustrated by German Torres

GRAPHIC UNIVERSE™ · MINNEAPOLIS · NEW YORK

Story by Evonne Tsang and Adan Jimenez

Pencils and inks by German Torres

Coloring by Marc Rueda

Lettering by Felix Ruiz

Copyright © 2012 by Lerner Publishing Group, Inc.

Graphic Universe™ and Twisted Journeys® are trademark of Lerner Publishing Group, Inc.

Graphic Universe™
A division of Lerner Publishing Group, Inc.
241 First Avenue North
Minneapolis, MN 55401 U.S.A.

Website address: www.lernerbooks.com

Main body text set in Myriad Tilt Bold 14/16. Typeface provided by Adobe Systems.

Library of Congress Cataloging-in-Publication Data

Tsang, Evonne.
      Hero city / by Evonne Tsang & Adan Jimenez ; illustrated by German Torres.
        p. cm. — (Twisted journeys ; #22)
      Summary: By choosing a specific page, will the reader, newly endowed with super powers, become a hero or a supervillain?
      ISBN: 978-0-7613-4595-4 (lib. bdg. : alk. paper)
      1. Plot-your-own stories. 2. Graphic novels. [1. Graphic novels. 2. Superheroes—Fiction.
3. Supervillains—Fiction. 4. Plot-your-own stories.] I. Jimenez, Adan, 1983– II. Torres, German, ill.
III. Title.
PZ7.7.T8He 2012
741.5'973—dc23
                                        2011051262

Manufactured in the United States of America
1 – DP – 7/15/12

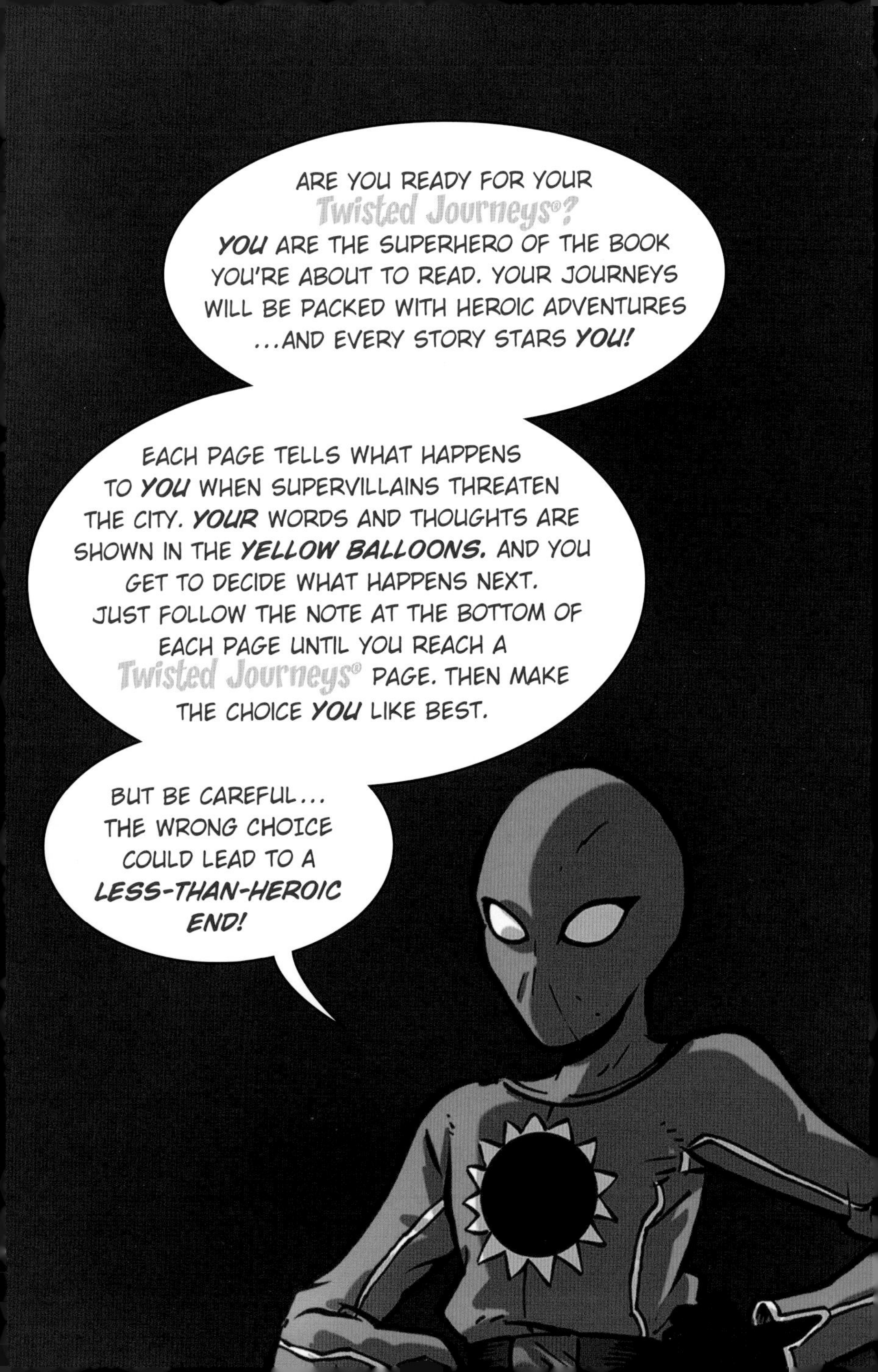
ARE YOU READY FOR YOUR Twisted Journeys®? YOU ARE THE SUPERHERO OF THE BOOK YOU'RE ABOUT TO READ. YOUR JOURNEYS WILL BE PACKED WITH HEROIC ADVENTURES ...AND EVERY STORY STARS YOU!
EACH PAGE TELLS WHAT HAPPENS TO YOU WHEN SUPERVILLAINS THREATEN THE CITY. YOUR WORDS AND THOUGHTS ARE SHOWN IN THE YELLOW BALLOONS. AND YOU GET TO DECIDE WHAT HAPPENS NEXT. JUST FOLLOW THE NOTE AT THE BOTTOM OF EACH PAGE UNTIL YOU REACH A Twisted Journeys® PAGE. THEN MAKE THE CHOICE YOU LIKE BEST.
BUT BE CAREFUL... THE WRONG CHOICE COULD LEAD TO A LESS-THAN-HEROIC END!

Pale sunlight fills your room early on a Monday morning as you get ready for the first day of school. It's a gloomy sort of day. You have your backpack ready to go when you notice an emergency news report on your television.

"There's been a breakout from Hart Island Prison," the reporter says, "the fortress where the city's worst metahuman criminals are locked up. These are dangerous criminals too powerful for normal prisons."

She adds, "And too powerful for Hart Island Prison too."

You turn up the sound so you can get every detail. "No information yet on how many prisoners are loose," the reporter goes on. "There are reports that the supervillain called Amsterdammerung is the mastermind behind the escape."

Hart Island Prison isn't far from where you live!

The reporter continues, "Authorities have requested help from metahuman heroes, but no one has seen Nightdragon or the Blue Squad yet. Their help will be needed to recapture the prisoners."

LIVE

NYZ HART ISLAND PRISON ESCAPE!

GO ON TO THE NEXT PAGE.

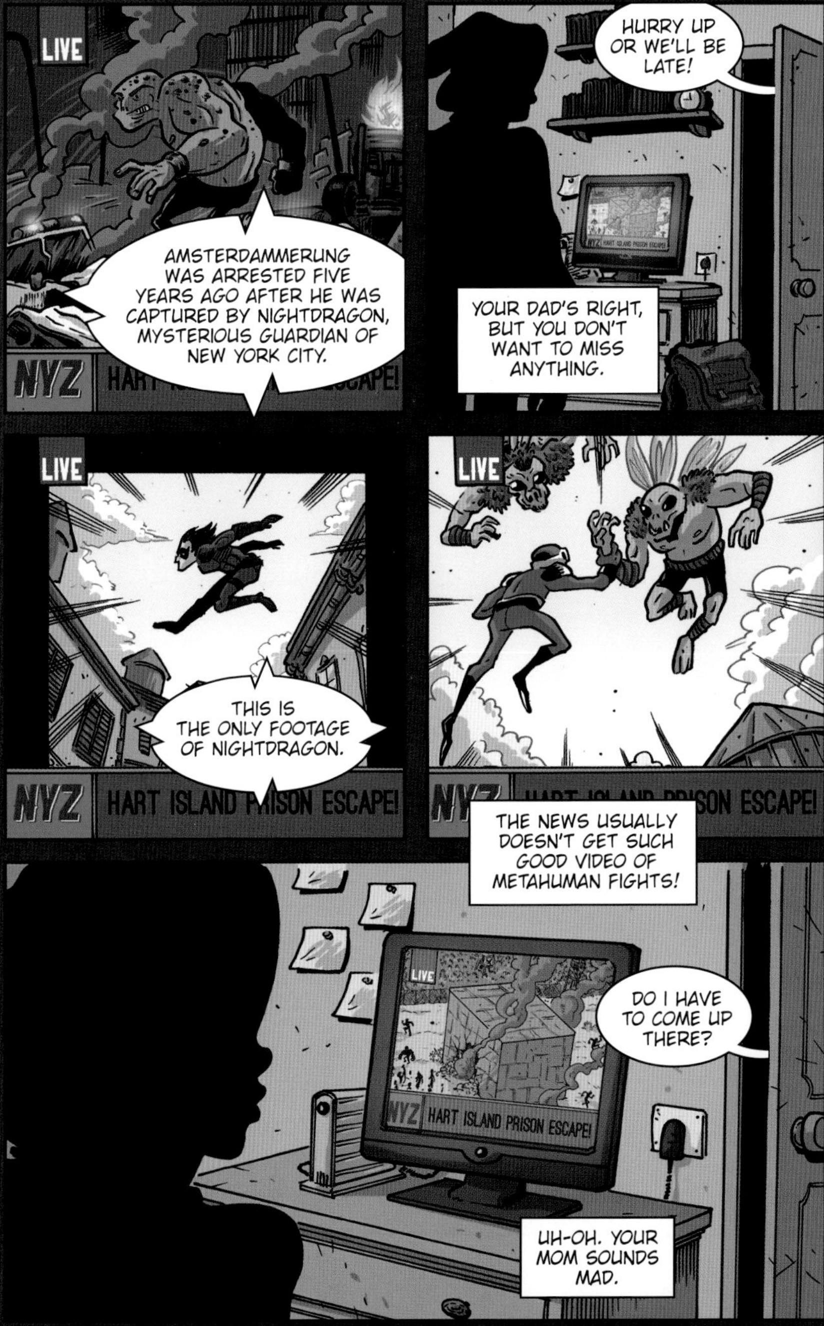
LIVE
AMSTERDAMMERUNG WAS ARRESTED FIVE YEARS AGO AFTER HE WAS CAPTURED BY NIGHTDRAGON, MYSTERIOUS GUARDIAN OF NEW YORK CITY.
NYZ
HURRY UP OR WE'LL BE LATE!
YOUR DAD'S RIGHT, BUT YOU DON'T WANT TO MISS ANYTHING.
LIVE
THIS IS THE ONLY FOOTAGE OF NIGHTDRAGON.
NYZ HART ISLAND PRISON ESCAPE!
LIVE
SON ESCAPE!
THE NEWS USUALLY DOESN'T GET SUCH GOOD VIDEO OF METAHUMAN FIGHTS!
LIVE
DO I HAVE TO COME UP THERE?
NYZ HART ISLAND PRISON ESCAPE!
UH-OH. YOUR MOM SOUNDS MAD.

GO ON TO THE NEXT PAGE.

TWISTED JOURNEYS®

You'll be late for school if you don't hurry.

WILL YOU . . .

. . . turn off the television and go downstairs?
TURN TO PAGE 89.

. . . watch a little longer in case
something good happens?
TURN TO PAGE 28.

Your badger nose can smell Greenwich's greenery when you leave the gym. You tell the others that you'll catch up, and you follow the scent.

"Wait!" Saratoga runs up to you and asks, "You're following that creep Greenwich, aren't you?"

You say, "Something about him bothers me. I know it's my first day . . ."

"Nah, you're right. He's totally suspicious looking. Must be your animal instincts. Greenwich is always sneaking off with Colonel Plum."

The scent leads you down to a basement level. Then the stink of chemicals makes it hard to track the plant smell, but you concentrate on following your knowledgeable nose.

It leads you to a sliding metal door with a keypad. It all looks very high tech. As you watch, the door *swoosh*es open and Greenwich steps out.

TURN TO PAGE 13.

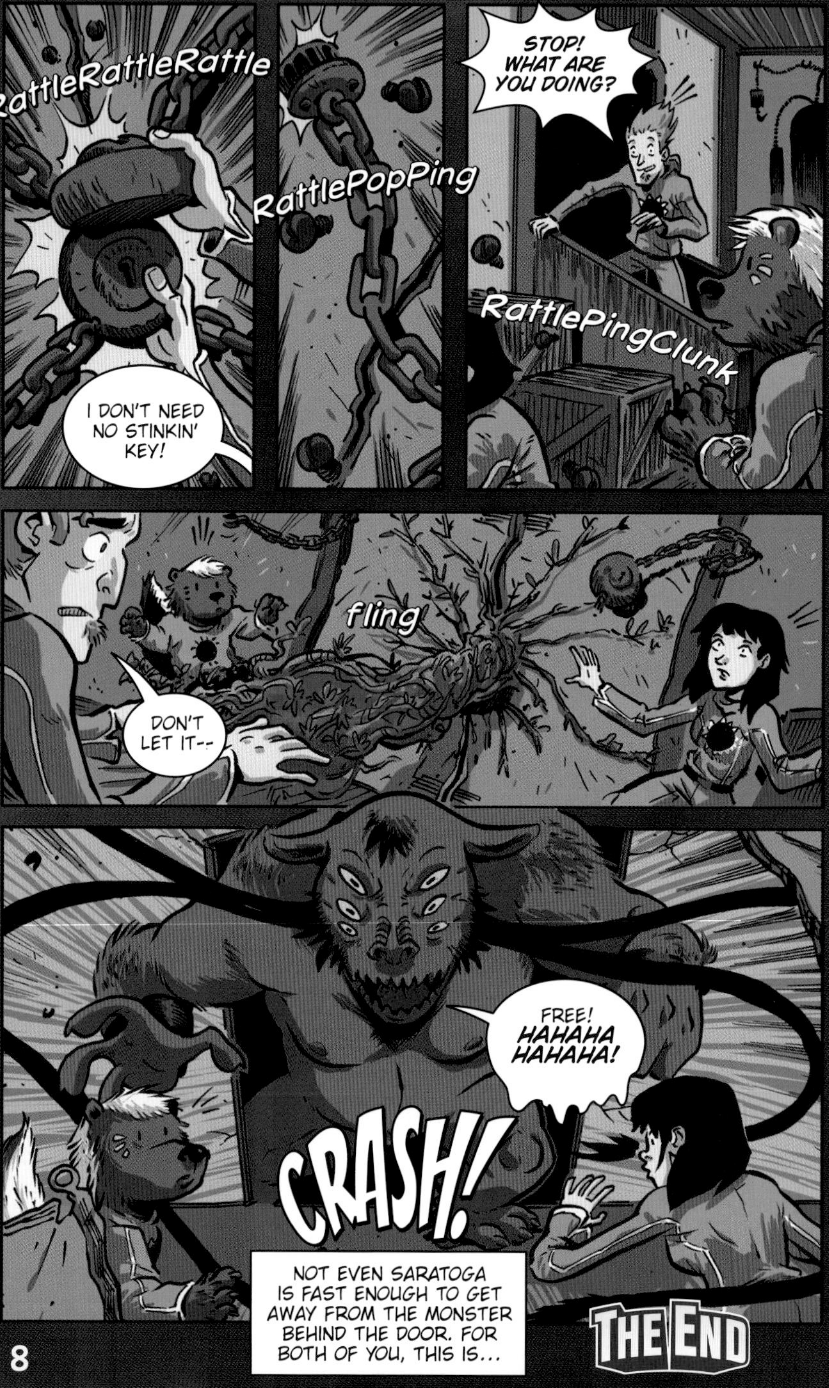
RattleRattleRattle
I DON'T NEED NO STINKIN' KEY!
RattlePopPing
STOP! WHAT ARE YOU DOING?
RattlePingClunk
fling
DON'T LET IT--
FREE! HAHAHA HAHAHA!
CRASH!
NOT EVEN SARATOGA IS FAST ENOUGH TO GET AWAY FROM THE MONSTER BEHIND THE DOOR. FOR BOTH OF YOU, THIS IS...
THE END

"I'm sorry, lady," you say, "but Osprey seemed really sure. Plus, he was hanging upside down."

"You're probably right," she says. "I just wanted a tall, dark, and handsome hero to chase me." She smiles at Nightdragon.

"There are lives at stake, Erytheia!" Nightdragon shouts. You and Nightdragon hop into the Dragonmobile and race to the Cloisters.

The Cloisters was created from parts of five French abbeys, to make a museum for some of the world's greatest medieval art. Then last summer it was the center of a superpowered battle. All the art that could be salvaged was moved out. The building was left as it was, a collapsing castle at the top of a hill.

"We'll go in quietly," whispers Nightdragon. "Stick close to me, and if you see the Terrier, give a shout."

GO ON TO THE NEXT PAGE.

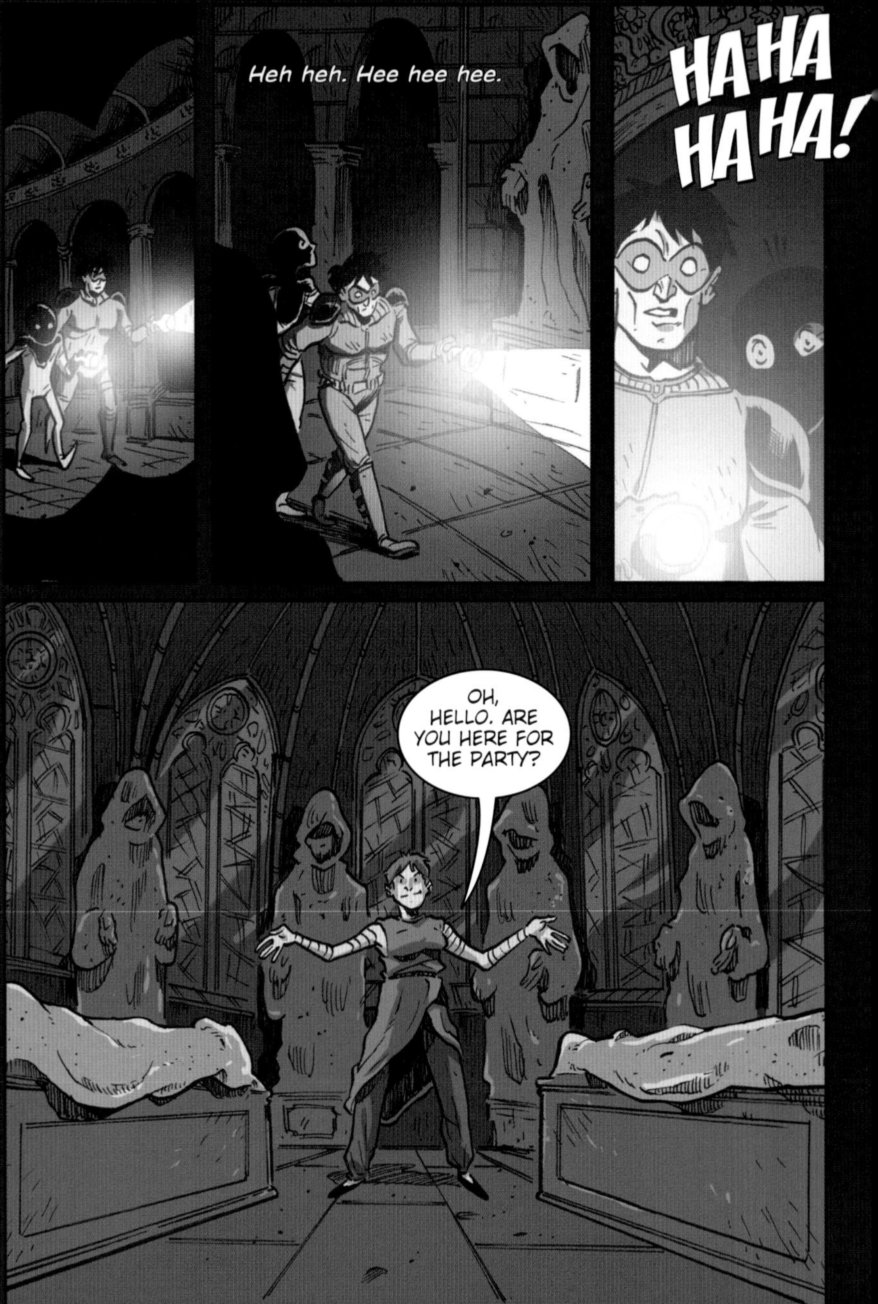
Heh heh. Hee hee hee.
HA HA HA HA HA!
OH, HELLO. ARE YOU HERE FOR THE PARTY?

GO ON TO THE NEXT PAGE.

"Terrier, what have you done?" Nightdragon yells.

You are completely numb when you see the figures lying still.

"My two new toys started squeaking too much." The Terrier cackles. She is smiling, but it doesn't hide how insane she is. "So I had to eliminate them."

"I am . . . I am so very sorry, Bluebird." Nightdragon puts his hand on your shoulder, but you can't feel it.

You let out a howl of rage and desperation, but your parents are gone, and you can't stop sobbing. You and Nightdragon easily capture the insane supervillainess, but bringing her to justice won't bring your parents back.

From that day forward, you become the city's fiercest crime fighter and avenger of evil.

THE END

Kid Empire says, "You're missing out on the fun." He leaves with Hayden.

Saratoga says, "I've seen Colonel Plum sneak huge boxes into his basement lab when the other teachers are away or late at night."

Then Saratoga looks around and whispers, "One time, the box had air holes, and there was a noise like something inside was alive."

That does sound pretty creepy, but you ask Saratoga, "How did you happen to see all this?"

"I'm pretty hyper and I don't need much sleep," she explains. "I get bored and run around a lot." In fact, Saratoga's hopping in place right now, as if it's hard for her to stand still.

It's a pretty wild story. You must look doubtful, because Saratoga says, "C'mon, let's check it out!"

GO ON TO THE NEXT PAGE.

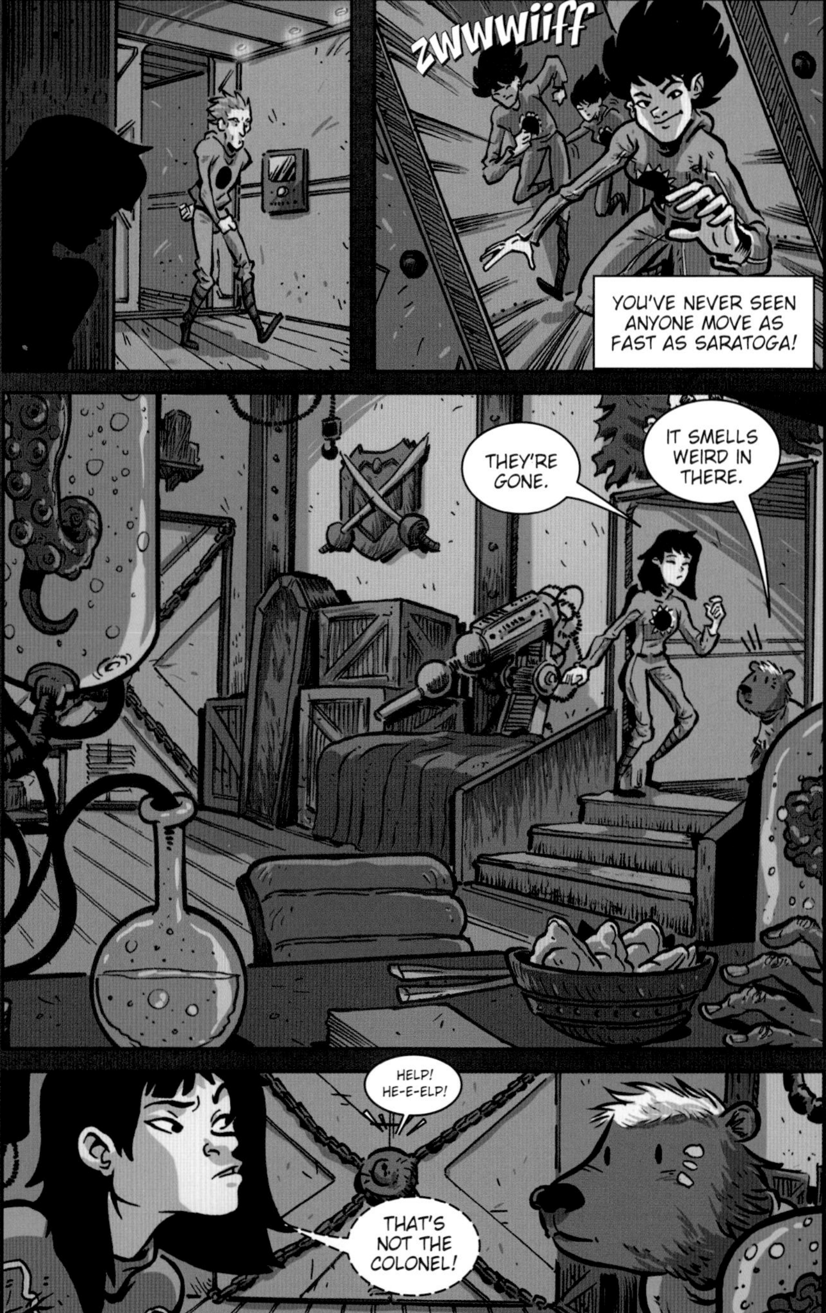
ZWWWIIFF
YOU'VE NEVER SEEN ANYONE MOVE AS FAST AS SARATOGA!
THEY'RE GONE.
IT SMELLS WEIRD IN THERE.
HELP! HE-E-ELP!
THAT'S NOT THE COLONEL!

GO ON TO THE NEXT PAGE.

TWISTED JOURNEYS®

You have no idea why this person's locked up. Maybe for being dangerous. But Colonel Plum does seem fishy.

WILL YOU . . .

. . . go find help?
TURN TO PAGE 34.

. . . try to free the prisoner?
TURN TO PAGE 8.

You meet your mom on the stairs. You start to say, "There's been a—"

An explosion hurls you down the stairs! The last thing you see is your mom trying to catch you.

When you open your eyes, you're in a plain room. A man is standing near you. He's glowing red. You hear his voice and realize it's your dad! He's on fire!

Without thinking, you run up and grab him. Your mom shouts, "Honey, no!"

Your dad tries to pull away. Now you see that he's not on fire—he has turned into lava! And your mom is so cold she's covered in ice!

Mom asks, "Are you hurt?"

It's weird. Even though your dad feels really hot, you aren't burned! He can't break your grip, either. You shakily ask, "What happened?"

A hippopotamus creature appears in an image projected on the wall. He says, "Welcome to Tamm World and Tweed's Tamm Many-Fights Arena! I am Tweed! If you want to go home, you must fight *many fights* for my audience's entertainment. What do you say?"

GO ON TO THE NEXT PAGE.

You don't even know how you ended up here!

WILL YOU AND YOUR FAMILY . . .

. . . agree to fight?
TURN TO PAGE 83.

. . . take the first chance to break out?
TURN TO PAGE 96.

Your dad shouts, "No! We won't fight for you anymore!"

Your mom shouts, "We refuse to fight kids!"

You swell with pride at their bravery.

Tweed suddenly announces, "Even I have a heart! Let's make a fresh start!" The arena erupts into cheers as soldiers lead you and the three kids off the field.

A lizard-headed man explains that your powers must be removed before you're sent home. There's something familiar about the medical pods he puts you in. The lid closes over you, and soon you drift into sleep. You never realize that you've been tricked. It's not your powers but your memories that are wiped clean.

The last thing you remember is that you were in your bedroom at home . . .

TURN TO PAGE 15.

You search the rows of buttons, knobs, and switches on the dashboard. You look back up at the viewscreen and see Cooper and Turner dragging Nightdragon across the room. You press one of the buttons, and Nightdragon's suit zaps both villains with 300 kilovolts of electrical shock.

They fall over, and Nightdragon shakes himself off and stands up. "I had this under control, Bluebird," he says, "but good thinking. You saved me the trouble of knocking them out myself."

Nightdragon looks down at Cooper and Turner. "Well, Bluebird, since you clearly can't stop touching my car, open the prison pod so I can put Turner in."

You find the controls to open the pod. Nightdragon tosses Turner in. "What about Cooper?" you ask.

"He's gonna tell us where your parents are."

GO ON TO THE NEXT PAGE.

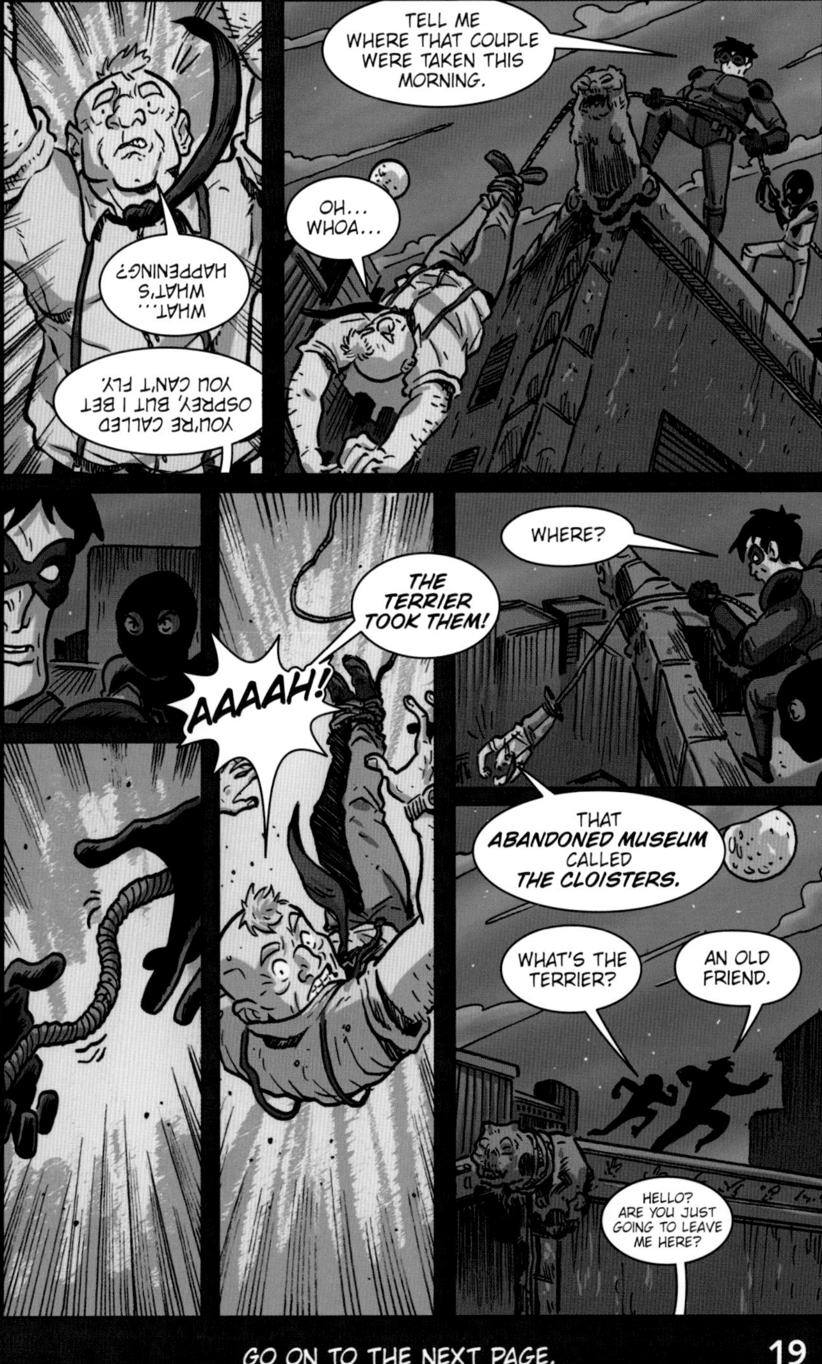
YOU'RE CALLED OSPREY, BUT I BET YOU CAN'T FLY.
WHAT... WHAT'S HAPPENING?
TELL ME WHERE THAT COUPLE WERE TAKEN THIS MORNING.
OH... WHOA...
THE TERRIER TOOK THEM!
AAAAH!
WHERE?
THAT ABANDONED MUSEUM CALLED THE CLOISTERS.
WHAT'S THE TERRIER?
AN OLD FRIEND.
HELLO? ARE YOU JUST GOING TO LEAVE ME HERE?

GO ON TO THE NEXT PAGE.

"No one knows who the Terrier really is," Nightdragon says. "But after her murder spree ten years ago, I started fighting crime."

Murder spree? A cold fear grips your heart. "If the Terrier has my parents, we have to find her as soon as possible!" You reach the Dragonmobile just as a girl dressed all in black swings down in front of it from the rooftops above.

"If you're looking for the Terrier, I can show you where she is."

"We already know where she is, Erytheia," Nightdragon says.

"You're going to trust that gangster?" the girl called Erytheia asks.

"Wait, who's this?" you ask.

"She's a thief," Nightdragon says.

"More like Robin Hood," Erytheia corrects him.

GO ON TO THE NEXT PAGE.

They're your parents, so you'll decide! Who's telling the truth? The gangster or the thief?

WILL YOU . . .

. . . head to the Cloisters?
TURN TO PAGE 9.

. . . follow Erytheia?
TURN TO PAGE 38

Tweed roars with rage and declares, "If that's how you feel, you can fight some other disobedient 'heroes'! Winners go free! But I'll destroy *all* of you if you refuse!"

A couple of rhino soldiers wheel the transporter gate into the arena to show that Tweed means what he says. Then three kids wearing matching uniforms are pushed into the arena too. Well, one of the kids actually looks like a badger. But the girl with the short dark hair . . .

She's *fast*. Before you even realize that she's moved, she's pushing you right across the arena. She's also whispering to you. "I'm Saratoga," she says. "My friends and I have an escape plan, but we need you guys to lose the fight. OK?" Then she zips back to her friends, so fast she's only a blur.

This is the chance you've been waiting for—if you can trust these strange kids.

22

GO ON TO THE NEXT PAGE.

TWISTED JOURNEYS®

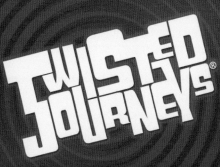

WILL YOU . . .

. . . convince your parents to go along with the plan?
TURN TO PAGE 78.

. . . refuse to fight again and all take a stand to defy Tweed together?
TURN TO PAGE 17.

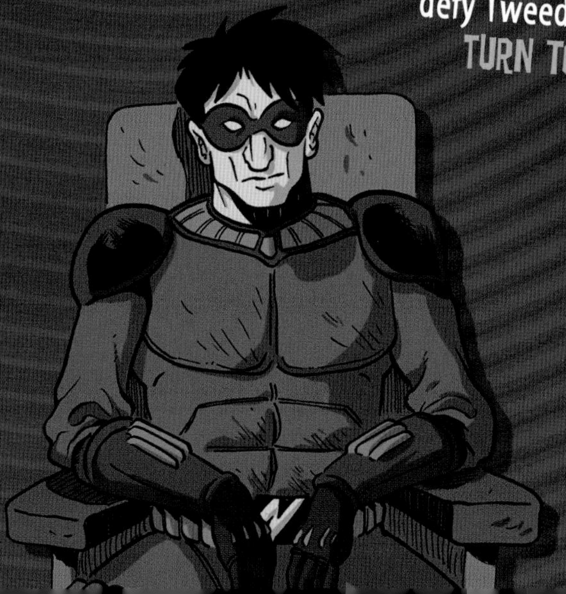

You use the rhino soldier's key card to get inside the building. You carry Nightdragon under one arm and Bluebird under the other while your parents knock out all the soldiers inside. The glowing transporter gate sits under the building's high, domed ceiling. The gate is still open to New York City, where they kidnapped Nightdragon and Bluebird.

Your parents return to normal as soon as they walk through the gate. When you step across, your arms give out and you drop Nightdragon and Bluebird—those guys are really heavy! You watch the portal nervously, but it closes behind you. Hopefully forever.

Nightdragon and Bluebird rest awhile, then disappear into the night. Your family happily heads home.

One evening, the doorbell rings. You follow your mom to the door and find Leonardo Ladon, famous billionaire owner of Night Tech Industries, and some girl. You realize who they must be and say, "Hey! You're—"

Nightdragon interrupts with a smile. "You're sharp, kid," he says. "Good thing my job offer to join my crime-fighting team includes your whole family."

THE END

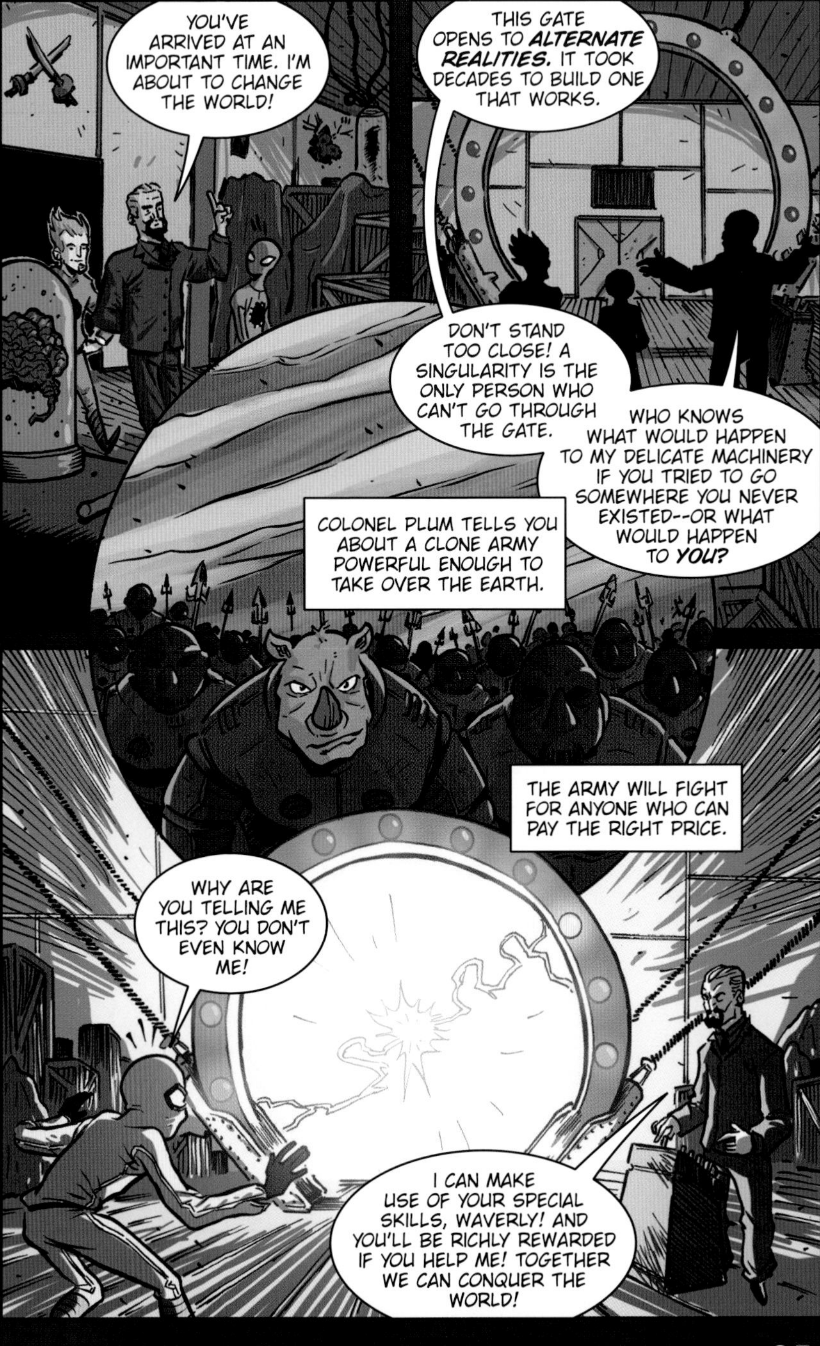

YOU'VE ARRIVED AT AN IMPORTANT TIME. I'M ABOUT TO CHANGE THE WORLD!
THIS GATE OPENS TO **ALTERNATE REALITIES.** IT TOOK DECADES TO BUILD ONE THAT WORKS.
DON'T STAND TOO CLOSE! A SINGULARITY IS THE ONLY PERSON WHO CAN'T GO THROUGH THE GATE.
WHO KNOWS WHAT WOULD HAPPEN TO MY DELICATE MACHINERY IF YOU TRIED TO GO SOMEWHERE YOU NEVER EXISTED--OR WHAT WOULD HAPPEN TO ***YOU?***
COLONEL PLUM TELLS YOU ABOUT A CLONE ARMY POWERFUL ENOUGH TO TAKE OVER THE EARTH.
THE ARMY WILL FIGHT FOR ANYONE WHO CAN PAY THE RIGHT PRICE.
WHY ARE YOU TELLING ME THIS? YOU DON'T EVEN KNOW ME!
I CAN MAKE USE OF YOUR SPECIAL SKILLS, WAVERLY! AND YOU'LL BE RICHLY REWARDED IF YOU HELP ME! TOGETHER WE CAN CONQUER THE WORLD!

GO ON TO THE NEXT PAGE.

As the Colonel speaks, you can almost see into the alternate futures before you.

WILL YOU . . .

. . . help Colonel Plum? You sense that his victory will bring you great power.

TURN TO PAGE 86.

. . . trick Colonel Plum? All you can see is pain and loneliness ahead.

TURN TO PAGE 70.

"Wait! I think I heard voices downstairs," you say. You look hopefully at Nightdragon, who stands as patient and still as a statue.

You nervously add, "I might recognize them if I heard them again."

Nightdragon seems to know you're lying, but he only says, "I'll find your parents as soon as I can."

With a step back into the shadows and the soft *whoosh* of a cape, Nightdragon is gone. You are bitterly disappointed, and things only get worse. The hospital releases you to your great-aunt Beatrice the next afternoon.

Aunt Beatrice is a terrible cook, and she keeps imagining terrible things happening to your parents.

Nightdragon does rescue your parents, but they don't remember anything that happened to them. Their kidnappers kept them knocked out with a sleep ray.

You're happy to be reunited with your parents, but they decide to move out to the country, far away from all your friends. They want to live where nothing bad happens. In fact, nothing ever happens there at all. It's worse than living with Aunt Beatrice.

THE END

School will have to wait. The news is showing an area that looks kind of familiar.

The reporters says, "Two of the escaped prisoners have been spotted in this area. The police are asking residents to stay in their homes."

It's your neighborhood! You hear sirens in the distance. Outside the window, helicopters zip past overhead.

Is that smoke down the street? You press your face against the window to see better, but a bright flash of light makes you jump back.

Suddenly, you hear your mom stomping up the stairs. She says, "You're going to be sorry I had to come back upstairs!"

Boy, your mom sounds mad. You think your parents must not know what's going on. Maybe they'll understand if you explain. Or your mom might even get angrier and not let you watch any more news.

GO ON TO THE NEXT PAGE.

WILL YOU . . .

. . . tell your parents what's going on?
TURN TO PAGE 15.

. . . lock your bedroom door to make sure you
don't miss anything?
TURN TO PAGE 46.

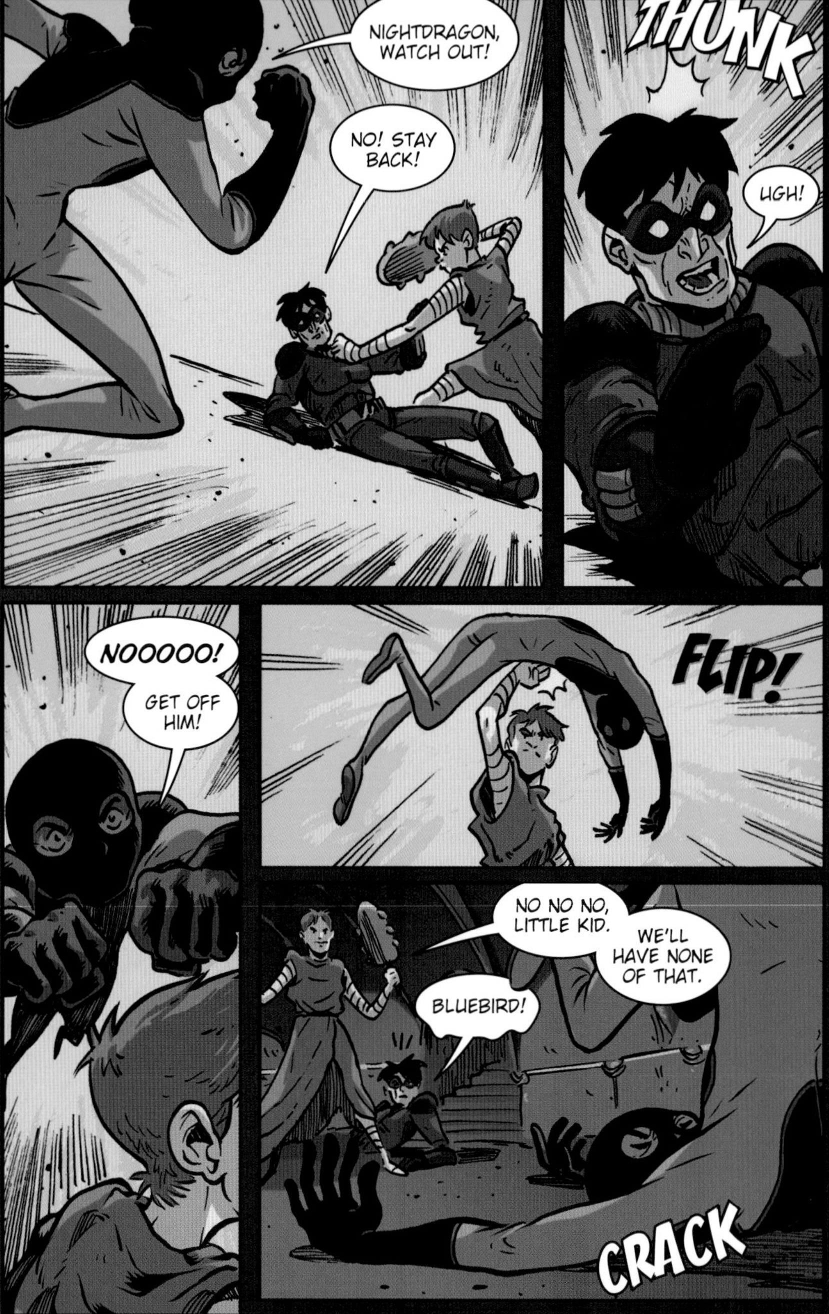
NIGHTDRAGON, WATCH OUT!
NO! STAY BACK!
THUNK
UGH!
NOOOOO!
GET OFF HIM!
FLIP!
NO NO NO, LITTLE KID.
WE'LL HAVE NONE OF THAT.
BLUEBIRD!
CRACK

GO ON TO THE NEXT PAGE.

Your ribs are burning. You think you've just broken a few.

The Terrier turns to look at Nightdragon, a maniacal grin on her face. "You've brought me another Bluebird? You gracious, gracious man! After I fed the last one to the sludge monster, I thought you would never let me play with another one again! I think I'll dispatch this one myself!"

The villainess creeps toward you, her dangerous club raised high. You can hardly breathe, let alone move, but Nightdragon is trying to stand up.

Someplace where you can't see her, Erytheia is screaming.

Nightdragon won't reach either one of you in time.

THE END

"I'm sorry," you say. "I was knocked out by the explosion. I didn't . . . I didn't see anything." You stifle a sob and whisper, "I can't help you at all."

Nightdragon stands as still as a statue for what seems like an eternity. Then he says, "One of my enemies took your parents as hostages, and you can help me find out who."

You nearly jump out of your bed with excitement. "Let's go!"

You and Nightdragon sneak out through an alley behind the hospital. There's a large car parked there. "Meet the Dragonmobile," Nightdragon explains, as if he's introducing you to an old friend. "I can't be everywhere at once, but this makes sure I can get anywhere quickly."

It's long and sinewy, with dragon motifs all over it and stylized wings on the sides. And the inside is so high tech!

"Tell me, what are you better at, in school?" Nightdragon asks. "Sports or science?"

GO ON TO THE NEXT PAGE.

Why would Nightdragon need to know this?

ARE YOU BETTER AT . . .

. . . sports?
TURN TO PAGE 73.

. . . science?
TURN TO PAGE 80.

"We don't know what's going on," you say. "We should get help."

Saratoga agrees, and the two of you hurry out of the lab. She dashes around a corner and you hear her gasp, "Colonel Plum!" Before you can reach the corner, you hear a horrifying scream.

You morph into a mouse and peek around the corner, but Saratoga is gone. You escape into a vent near the floor. You manage to find a group of students and look innocent when Colonel Plum shows up, looking for Saratoga's accomplices. He seems satisfied that Saratoga was alone.

No trace of Saratoga is ever found. Colonel Plum increases security so that it's impossible to get near his lab again. You don't know who else is on Colonel Plum's side, so you keep your secret to yourself.

All you can do for now is learn to use your superpower. You carefully watch Colonel Plum and swear to avenge Saratoga someday.

THE END

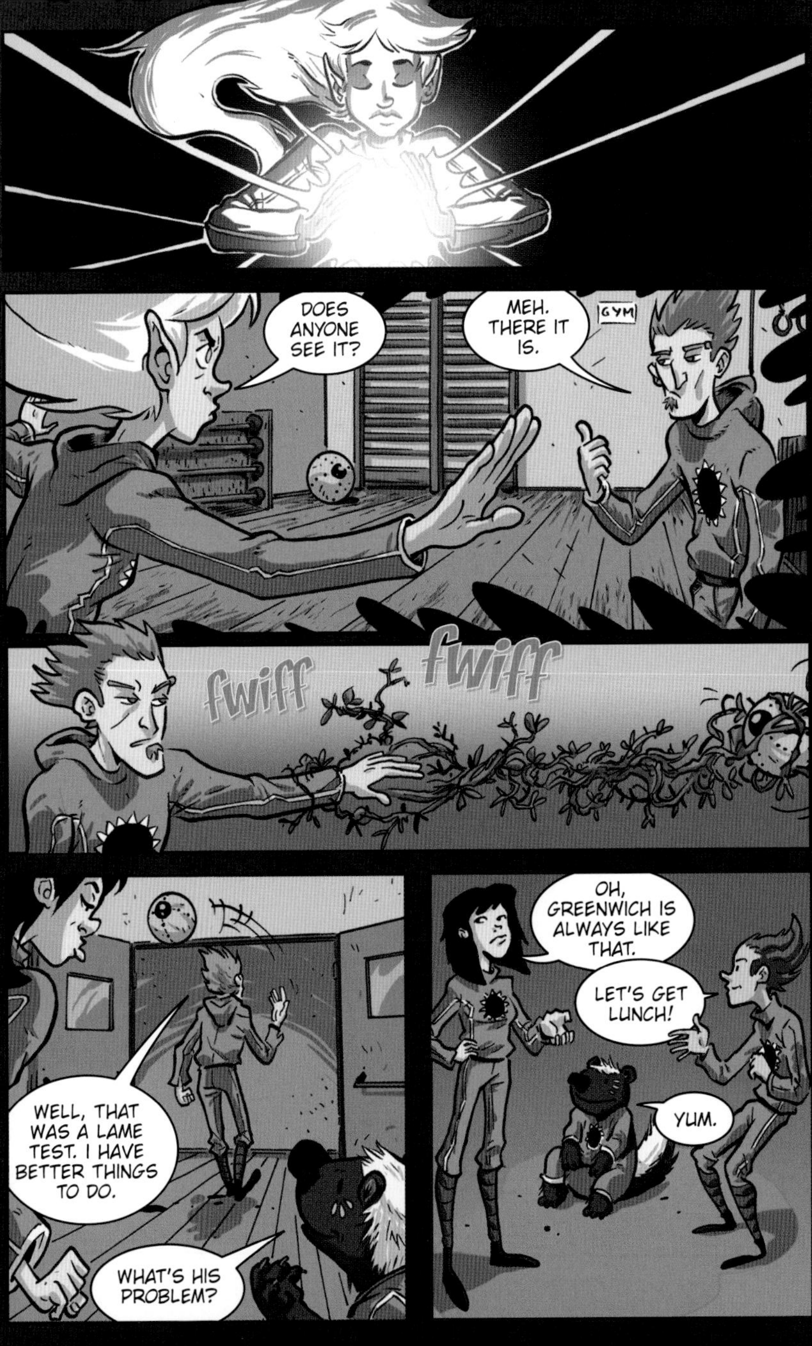
DOES ANYONE SEE IT?
MEH. THERE IT IS.
GYM
fwiff
fwiff
WELL, THAT WAS A LAME TEST. I HAVE BETTER THINGS TO DO.
WHAT'S HIS PROBLEM?
OH, GREENWICH IS ALWAYS LIKE THAT.
LET'S GET LUNCH!
YUM.

GO ON TO THE NEXT PAGE.

WILL YOU . . .

. . . give in to curiosity and follow Greenwich?
TURN TO PAGE 7.

. . . join your new friends for lunch?
TURN TO PAGE 106.

It's easy to herd the unsuspecting students into the practice room. Greenwich reprograms Minetta's sensors to neutralize everyone's powers and lock them in the room. Maybe you feel a little pity when everyone is forced through the gate. You know that Tweed will harvest their powers to make his troops even deadlier.

But you forget them soon enough, as Colonel Plum begins conquering the world with his alien army. With you at his side to see the future and help with every decision, Colonel Plum is unstoppable.

By the time you're an adult, Colonel Plum rules most of the world. You live a life of luxury, with everything you've ever wanted. Colonel Plum has proven loyal, and you and Greenwich rule alongside him. The three of you are respected—or feared—by every person on Earth.

You sometimes sense that in the future, only one of you will be the supreme ruler. For now, it's just something to dream about. And plan for.

THE END

"Nightdragon, why would she lie about this?" you ask.

Nightdragon sighs. "She has no reason to. She's a thief, but she's never actually hurt anyone."

"Then let's go after your parents, kid!" says Erytheia.

It's a tight squeeze, but all three of you get into the Dragonmobile. Erytheia directs you to the abandoned City Hall subway station.

You jump the fence into the grounds and sneak through a grove of dogwood trees. Erytheia leads you to a concrete slab on the ground. It has a smashed-through window in the center.

"See?" Erytheia says. "Two parents and one lunatic villain, one floor down."

She produces a rope, and the three of you climb down.

GO ON TO THE NEXT PAGE.

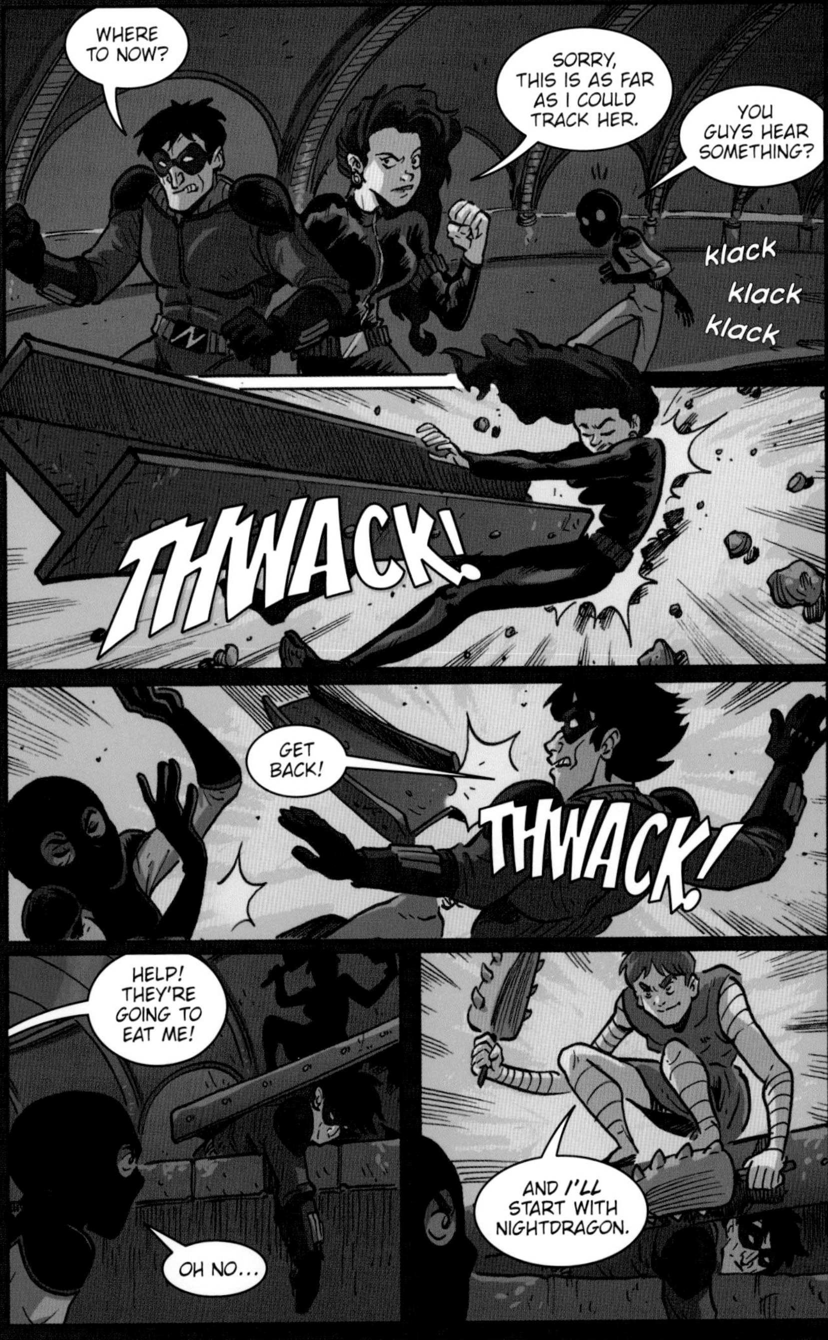
WHERE TO NOW?
SORRY, THIS IS AS FAR AS I COULD TRACK HER.
YOU GUYS HEAR SOMETHING?
klack
klack
klack
THWACK!
GET BACK!
THWACK!
HELP! THEY'RE GOING TO EAT ME!
OH NO...
AND I'LL START WITH NIGHTDRAGON.

GO ON TO THE NEXT PAGE.

WHO WILL YOU HELP FIRST?

...Nightdragon?
TURN TO PAGE 30.

...Erytheia?
TURN TO PAGE 93.

"Why do these bills have a weird face on them?"

"Those belonged to my enemy Wall Street," Nightdragon explains. "He prints money with his face on it, demanding that it be used as the only legal currency in the world."

"That's ludi—" A huge explosion rocks the Dragon's Lair before you can finish your sentence!

An enormous turtle-shaped machine with a drill for a snout punches through one of the walls. A hatch opens up on top, and two men climb out.

"Wall Street! Turtle! How did you find my lair?" Nightdragon shouts.

"I knew that when I kidnapped this kid's parents, you would visit the kid." The villainous Wall Street snickers. "With the Turtle's digging machine, we could follow you without being detected!"

"Gawp!" Turtle agrees.

Five henchmen in green turtleneck sweaters emerge from inside the machine, holding your tied-up parents!

"I'll take the Turtlenecks," Nightdragon tells you. "You save your parents."

GO ON TO THE NEXT PAGE.

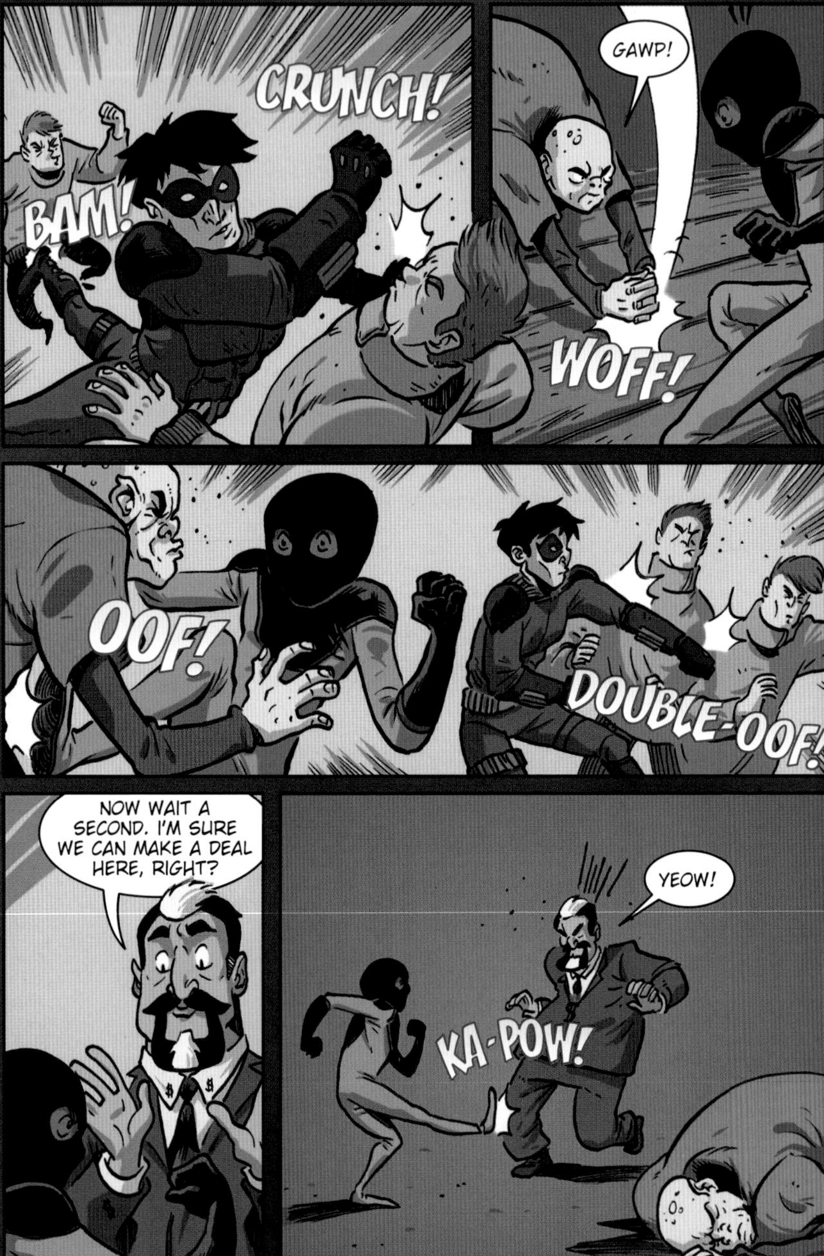
CRUNCH!
BAM!
GAWP!
WOFF!
OOF!
DOUBLE-OOF!
NOW WAIT A SECOND. I'M SURE WE CAN MAKE A DEAL HERE, RIGHT?
YEOW!
KA-POW!

GO ON TO THE NEXT PAGE.

"Dang it, Turtle! I paid you for your muscle!" Wall Street shouts, rubbing his shin.

"You get what you pay for, Wall Street," Nightdragon responds, punching out the last Turtleneck. "Fake money will always get you fake service."

"Gawp . . ." agrees the Turtle.

You run to your parents and hug them tight. "Mom! Dad! Are you OK?"

"Honey, is that you?" your mom asks. "We're OK, but why are you dressed like this?"

Uh-oh. "Nightdragon," you say, "these bad guys know your secret hideout, and even worse, my parents know I'm Bluebird!"

"Don't worry, chum," Nightdragon says. "I have a Basilisk Blackout machine."

"You have a machine that will make them all forget? That's ludi—"

"Don't touch my suit, Nightdragon!" Wall Street yells as Nightdragon cuffs him. "That's expensive material!"

"You should know more than most, Wall Street, that crime never pays. And it always wrinkles your suit."

"Gawp . . ." agrees the Turtle.

THE END

"I wish we had a guide," says your mom as you sneak along the street.

An arena door opens, and a lizard-headed man walks out. He's reading some sort of tablet and doesn't see you.

Your dad stands on the creature's left. Your mom stands on his right. You stand in front of him. He glares at you and snaps, "I'm Tweed's personal advisor! How dare you!"

You say, "I bet you know how we can get back home!"

Suddenly, he looks nervous. "I know nothing!"

"Then we should just silence you," says your dad, raising a fiery hand.

You can't believe the lizard man believes the threat, but it's a good thing he does! He changes his tune and says that he can take you to the transporter gate.

He sneaks you into a walled yard with many buildings around it. You see a door open in a big, domed structure. A soldier comes out, pushing a pod-shaped medical gurney. From the distance, it looks as if there are two unconscious humans in the pod.

"We must hurry or we'll be seen," hisses the lizard man.

GO ON TO THE NEXT PAGE.

Should you risk losing your chance to go home, to help two strangers?

WILL YOU . . .

. . . rescue the other humans?
TURN TO PAGE 99.

. . . follow the lizard man to the transporter?
TURN TO PAGE 111.

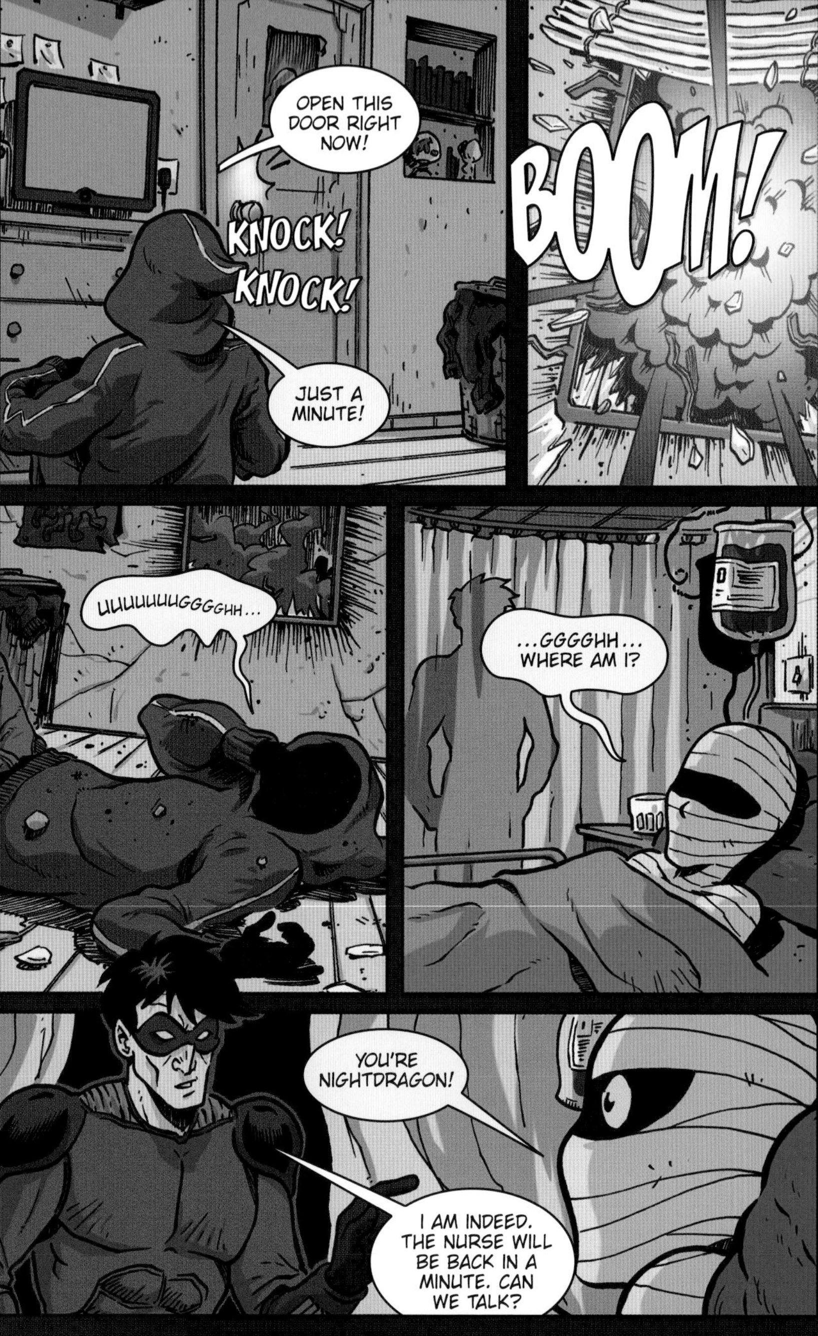
OPEN THIS DOOR RIGHT NOW!
KNOCK! KNOCK!
JUST A MINUTE!
BOOM!
UUUUUUUGGGGHH...
...GGGGHH... WHERE AM I?
YOU'RE NIGHTDRAGON!
I AM INDEED. THE NURSE WILL BE BACK IN A MINUTE. CAN WE TALK?

GO ON TO THE NEXT PAGE.

You can't believe Nightdragon is talking to you! His voice is very deep and a little scary. Then it's as if you wake up for real. You're in the hospital. Something bad must have happened.

You ask Nightdragon, "Where are my parents? Are they waiting outside?"

Nightdragon says, "I'm sorry. Your parents were kidnapped by escaped prisoners. I'm trying to find them. Do you remember anything about the attack?"

You stare at him in shock. You tell Nightdragon that you saw the flash down the street, and then you fall silent. You realize that you may never see your parents again and the last thing you did was lock your door against them.

Nightdragon sees that you're upset and says, "You need rest. Is there anything else before I go?"

You start to explain and then pause. If you confess that you didn't see anything, Nightdragon will just leave and you'll probably never get to talk to him again.

GO ON TO THE NEXT PAGE.

You'd better talk fast before Nightdragon leaves.

WILL YOU . . .

. . . make up something to keep him there?
TURN TO PAGE 27.

. . . confess that you locked the door and were knocked out by the explosion?
TURN TO PAGE 32.

You search the rows of buttons, knobs, and switches, and then figure out how to press three in a row to open the cockpit. You rush up the fire escape to the window and peek in.

"Won't he just put you in jail when he wakes up?" Turner asks.

"Not if I send him there first," says Cooper. "Remember, he broke in. I was defending myself." Cooper heads for the door. "Watch him while I call the cops. If he wakes up, thwack him again."

Turner chuckles. "Sure thing, boss."

After Cooper leaves, Turner sits down next to Nightdragon—who immediately reaches up and slams Turner's head into the floor, knocking him out.

"Nightdragon! You're OK!" You climb in through the window.

GO ON TO THE NEXT PAGE.

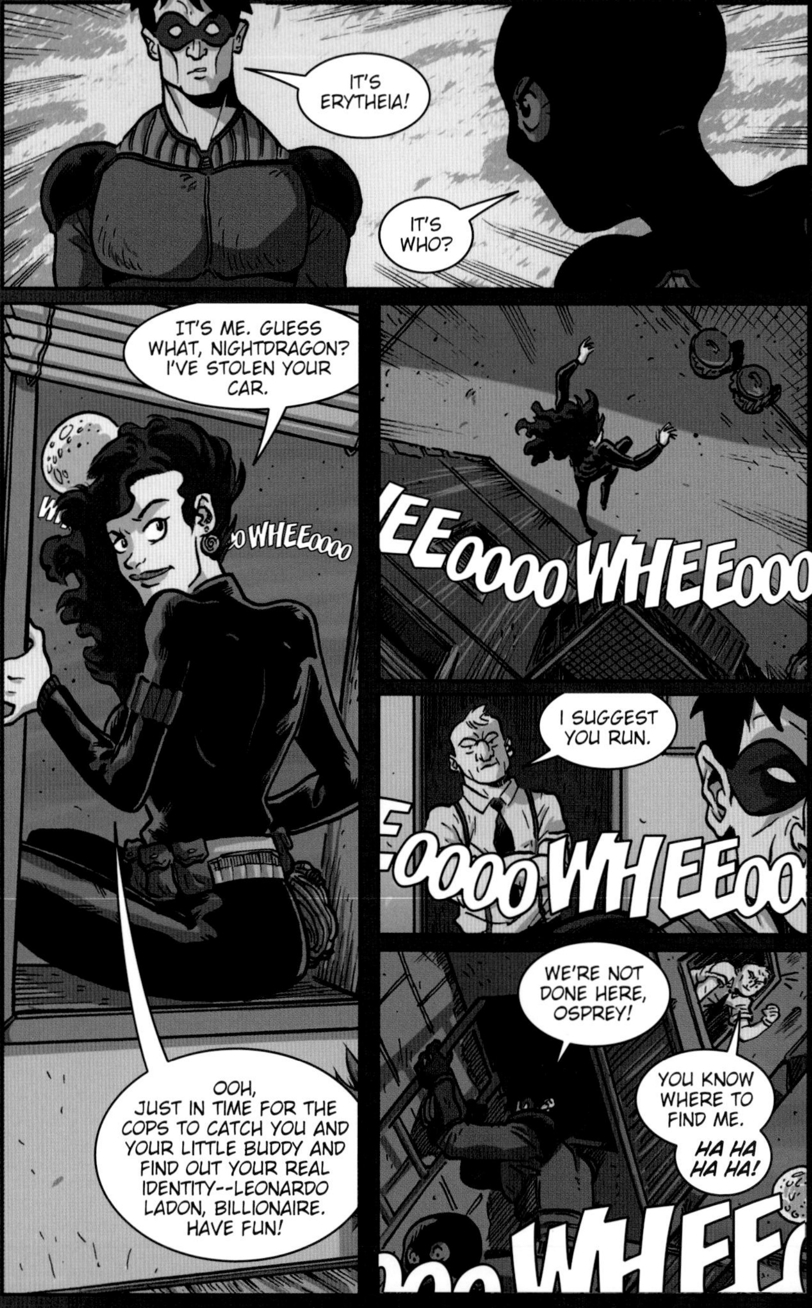

IT'S ERYTHEIA!
IT'S WHO?
IT'S ME. GUESS WHAT, NIGHTDRAGON? I'VE STOLEN YOUR CAR.
WHEEoooo
OOH, JUST IN TIME FOR THE COPS TO CATCH YOU AND YOUR LITTLE BUDDY AND FIND OUT YOUR REAL IDENTITY--LEONARDO LADON, BILLIONAIRE. HAVE FUN!
EEoooo WHEEoooo
I SUGGEST YOU RUN.
oooo WHEEoo
WE'RE NOT DONE HERE, OSPREY!
YOU KNOW WHERE TO FIND ME.
HA HA HA HA!

GO ON TO THE NEXT PAGE.

You follow Nightdragon across the rooftops, as police helicopters get nearer. "Who was that?"

"My archnemesis! And I told you to stay in the car!" Nightdragon scolds you as he runs.

You can't keep up with him. "You were in trouble!" you protest.

Nightdragon jumps across a gap too wide for you. "I'll find your parents for you. The police will take care of you until then."

He races away across the rooftops, leaving you behind. A police helicopter spots you and tells you to freeze. When the police take you in, you tell them everything that happened to you.

The next day, Nightdragon rescues your parents from a lunatic supervillain who broke out of Hart Island, and the police let you go home.

Days pass, then weeks, then months. Life returns to normal. But you never forget the one day that you were Bluebird, a hero's sidekick . . . and let a thief steal the Dragonmobile.

THE END

"Nightdragon!" you whisper. "I found my parents. They're under guard."

"Good job, Bluebird!" comes a voice from the earpiece. "I'm on my way!"

Nightdragon arrives shortly and says, "I'll knock out the guards, and you untie your parents. Keep your eyes open, because we could get an avalanche of more Snowmen at any moment."

Nightdragon swoops in and attacks the two henchmen. You rush over to your parents. "Citizens, please do not be alarmed!" you say, disguising your voice. "I'm Bluebird, Nightdragon's new partner!"

Your parents look scared but unharmed. You start untying them while Nightdragon finishes up with the Snowmen, but before you're done, Snowstorm himself slides into view!

And he has another Popsicle of Power!

"Where do you think you're going with my guests, Nightdragon?" he shouts, cackling. "They haven't finished their snow peas or iced teas yet!" Snowstorm skids across the ice rink. You and Nightdragon leap after him—and land in the middle of a gang of his ice-skating Snowmen henchmen.

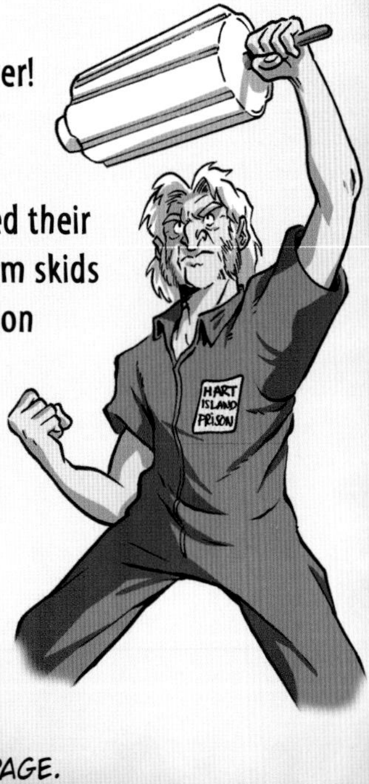
HART ISLAND PRISON

GO ON TO THE NEXT PAGE.

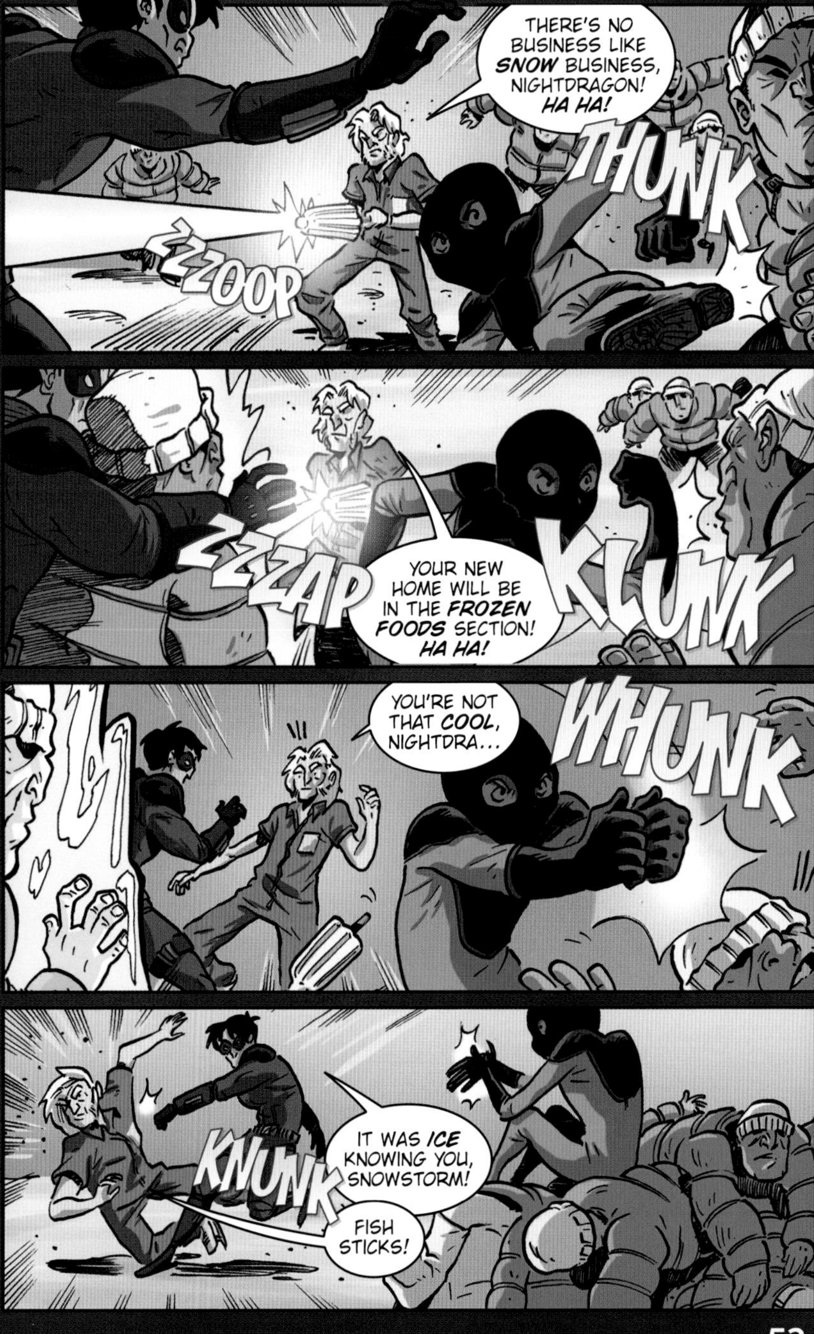
THERE'S NO BUSINESS LIKE SNOW BUSINESS, NIGHTDRAGON! HA HA!
THUNK
ZZZOOP
ZZZAP
YOUR NEW HOME WILL BE IN THE FROZEN FOODS SECTION! HA HA!
KLUNK
YOU'RE NOT THAT COOL, NIGHTDRA...
WHUNK
IT WAS ICE KNOWING YOU, SNOWSTORM!
KNUNK
FISH STICKS!

GO ON TO THE NEXT PAGE.

"That pun was awful," you tell Nightdragon.

"It's the only language scum like this understands, Bluebird."

The police arrive soon after the fight and arrest everybody, including Snowstorm. Nightdragon tells you to hurry home and hide your costume. He will bring your parents back home after they give their statement to the police.

A few hours later, your parents come home. "Mom! Dad!" you exclaim, giving them both hugs. "I was so worried! Are you OK?"

"We're fine," your dad says. "Nightdragon saved us from Snowstorm!"

You pretend to be surprised. "What?"

"Oh sweetie, you should have seen it!" your mom says. "And I think his new sidekick might have been even better than Nightdragon!"

"Really?" you say, an enormous grin spreading across your face. "Tell me everything."

THE END

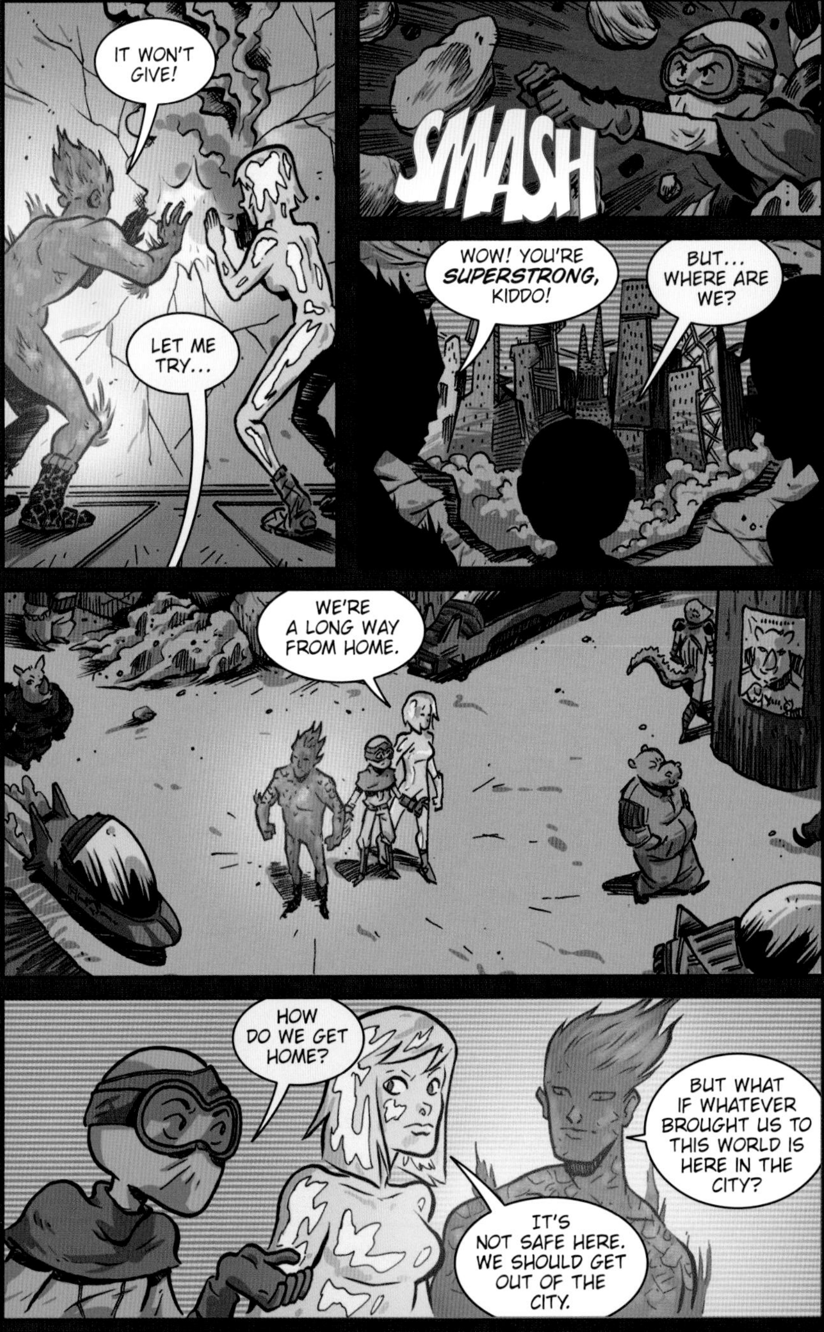
IT WON'T GIVE!
LET ME TRY...
SMASH
WOW! YOU'RE SUPERSTRONG, KIDDO!
BUT... WHERE ARE WE?
WE'RE A LONG WAY FROM HOME.
HOW DO WE GET HOME?
IT'S NOT SAFE HERE. WE SHOULD GET OUT OF THE CITY.
BUT WHAT IF WHATEVER BROUGHT US TO THIS WORLD IS HERE IN THE CITY?

GO ON TO THE NEXT PAGE.

You need to get moving before anyone realizes
that you've escaped.

WILL YOU . . .

. . . get out of the city for now?
TURN TO PAGE 62.

. . . look for a way home inside the city?
TURN TO PAGE 44.

You and your parents race after the lizard man. You'll go back for Nightdragon and Bluebird, his trusty sidekick, after you catch the advisor.

Just when you think he's gone, your mom sees him dashing around a corner. You turn the corner and stop in surprise.

It's a trap! The lizard man stands behind a row of guards with laser weapons pointed at you. More soldiers run in behind you, leaving you with no escape.

The advisor shouts, "Fire!" You leap in front of your parents to protect them with your superstrength. Yellow energy beams wash over you.

Nothing happens.

Then you look at your parents and realize that the yellow beams have turned them back to normal. That must mean that none of you has superpowers anymore!

"Fire disintegration beams!" shouts the lizard man. All you and your family can do is hug one another as the second wave of lasers brings . . .

THE END

"Why doesn't this popsicle melt?" you ask.

"This is the Popsicle of Power," Nightdragon explains, "one of the many wintry weapons I have taken from my frozen foe, Snowstorm. He escaped from Hart Island this morning."

"How could a popsicle possibly be a weapon?" you wonder.

"I know it looks harmless," Nightdragon replies, "but trust me, that thing can freeze—and then explode—anything."

"Could something like that have blown up my street this morning?" you ask.

"It's certainly possible," the cloaked crime fighter says. "Let's go shake some evergreen trees and see if any snow falls out."

You follow Nightdragon to an elevator. "Hold on," he warns.

The elevator rockets to life, and you clutch the handrail. The elevator speeds first one direction and then another. You're pulled and pushed this way and that. The elevator stops just as suddenly as it started. You stumble out and find yourself on a rooftop overlooking the city.

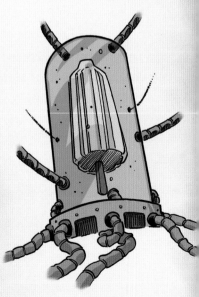

GO ON TO THE NEXT PAGE.

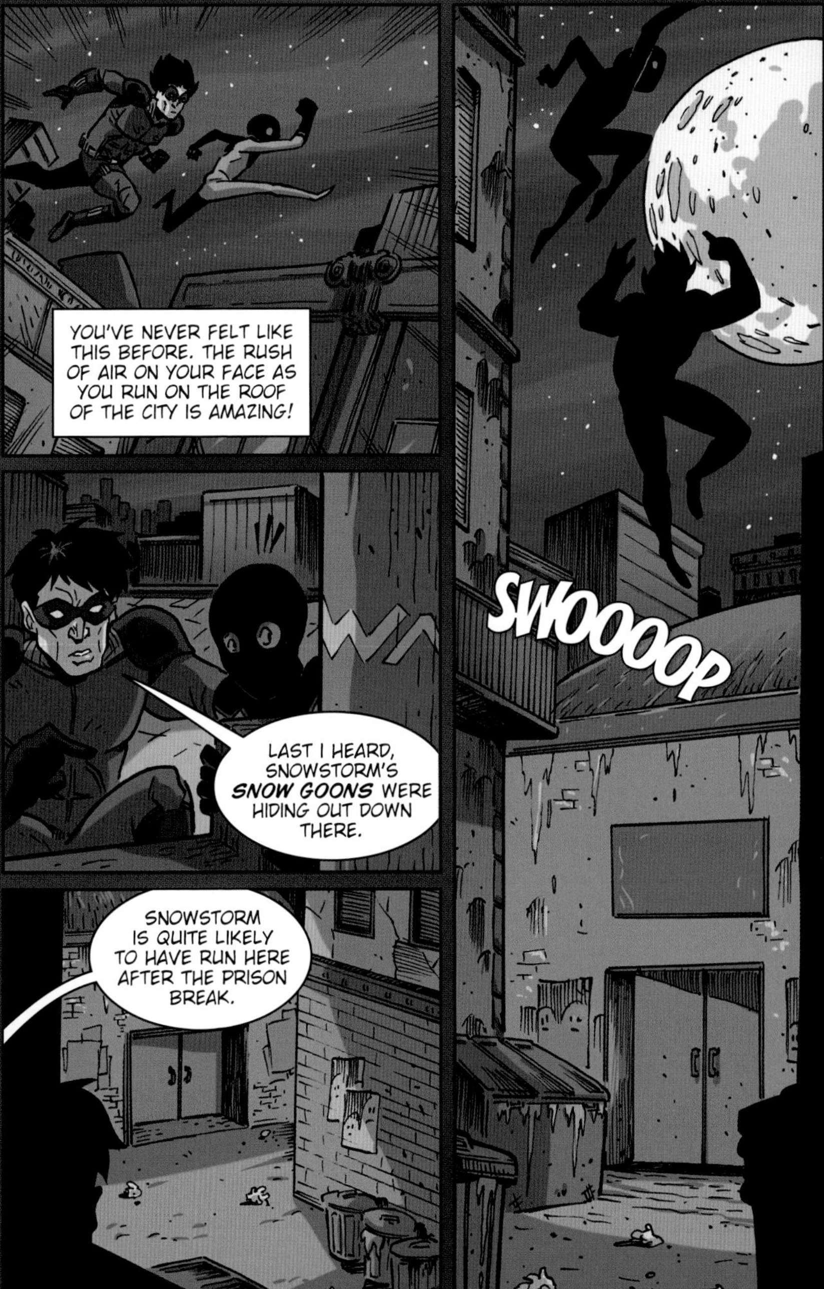
YOU'VE NEVER FELT LIKE THIS BEFORE. THE RUSH OF AIR ON YOUR FACE AS YOU RUN ON THE ROOF OF THE CITY IS AMAZING!
LAST I HEARD, SNOWSTORM'S SNOW GOONS WERE HIDING OUT DOWN THERE.
SNOWSTORM IS QUITE LIKELY TO HAVE RUN HERE AFTER THE PRISON BREAK.
SWOOOOP

GO ON TO THE NEXT PAGE.

When you reach the ground, Nightdragon warns you, "Be very, very quiet. If we can sneak in, it'll be a lot easier to locate Snowstorm."

You follow Nightdragon into the ice rink offices. He motions for you to crouch low as you walk. The offices all seem empty.

Nightdragon whispers, "We'll cover more ground if we split up. But if you spot any of Snowstorm's Snowmen henchmen, do not engage. Hide and report back to me with this."

He hands you a small earpiece. "Put it in your ear and whisper your location. I'll be able to hear you clearly and track you."

Nightdragon goes left while you turn right. You walk on softly for a while, crouching down. Then you suddenly hear voices from the rink. You sneak closer and see two guys who must be Snowstorm's henchmen. Two people are lying nearby, tied up and unconscious.

The henchmen are guarding your parents!

GO ON TO THE NEXT PAGE.

Your parents need help fast!

WILL YOU . . .

. . . call Nightdragon for help using the earpiece?
TURN TO PAGE 52.

. . . rush in and take the two guards by surprise?
TURN TO PAGE 85.

Most of the citizens must be at the arena, because there aren't many people around. It's easy to avoid being seen. You run down back alleys and hide when you hear soldiers looking for you. You reach the edge of town and duck under a huge, arched structure that your mom calls an aqueduct, a channel for bringing water to a city.

Suddenly, a kid pops out from behind a pillar. She has long white hair and eyes that glitter like a starry night. She waves and says, "Hi. I bet you're confused right now."

Your dad moves protectively in front of you and asks, "Who are you?"

"I'm called Hayden," the girl explains. "Tweed kidnapped me too. No one has found the way off this world yet. But we're using the superpowers he gave us to fight him and get everyone home. Interested?"

You and your parents decide to join up. Over the years, you meet people from different worlds who become like family. And you never give up hope of finding a way home.

THE END

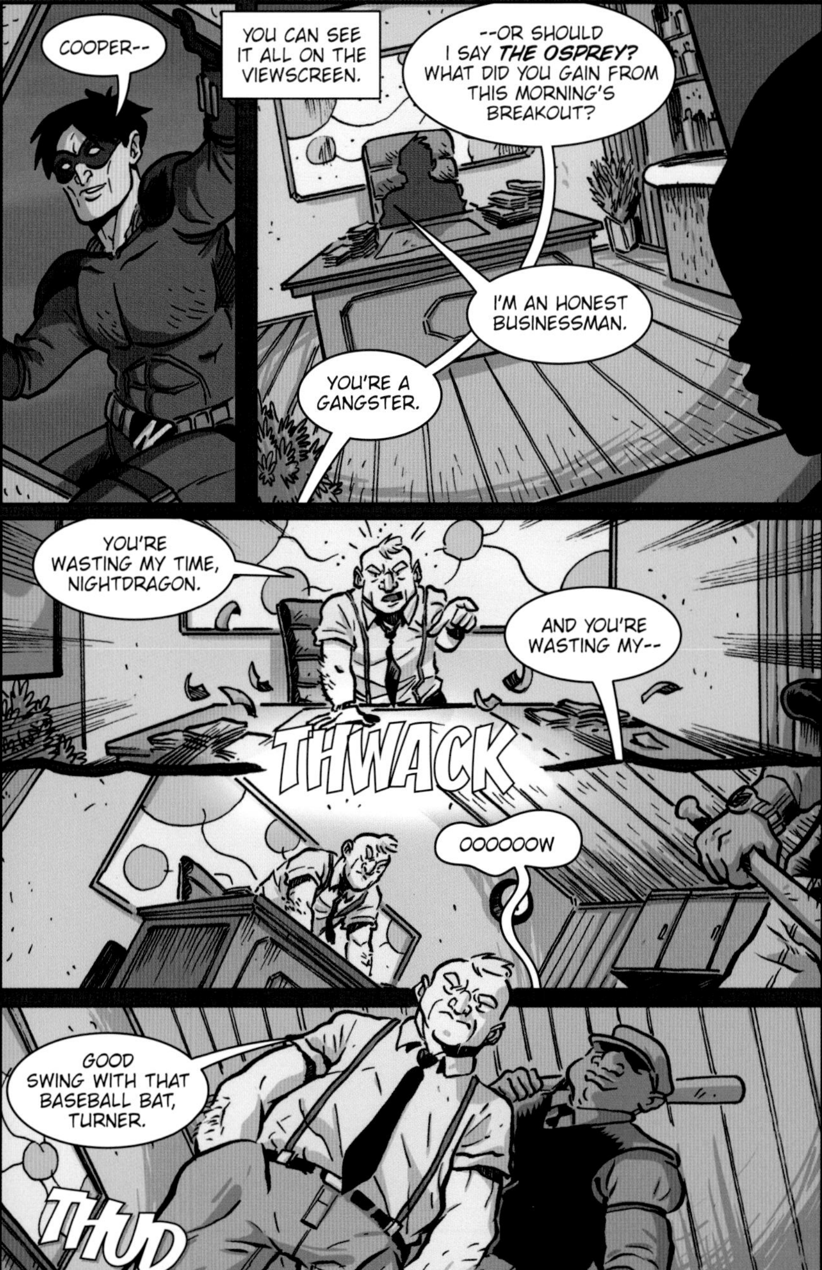

COOPER--
YOU CAN SEE IT ALL ON THE VIEWSCREEN.
--OR SHOULD I SAY ***THE OSPREY?*** WHAT DID YOU GAIN FROM THIS MORNING'S BREAKOUT?
I'M AN HONEST BUSINESSMAN.
YOU'RE A GANGSTER.
YOU'RE WASTING MY TIME, NIGHTDRAGON.
AND YOU'RE WASTING MY--
THWACK
OOOOOOW
GOOD SWING WITH THAT BASEBALL BAT, TURNER.
THUD

Nightdragon needs your help, but he's locked you in the Dragonmobile!

WILL YOU . . .

. . . try to get out and help?
TURN TO PAGE 49.

. . . try to help somehow from inside the car?
TURN TO PAGE 18.

The gym is underground and as big as an airplane hangar. Curving up to the ceiling are huge support pillars covered in pulsing globes. More globes float near every student.

"What are those?" you ask.

Hayden explains. "They're sensors. It's how Minetta monitors us when we use our powers. If he has to, he can use them to neutralize our powers and make sure we stay safe. Haven't you met Minetta? Minetta, say hello to Moreau!"

"Hello, Moreau. Welcome to the Ellis Academy." The voice seems to come from everywhere.

You look around, but you can't see who is speaking. "Hello?" you call. "Where are you?"

Minetta answers, "I am the academy's automated operational system. I monitor and regulate everything from the electricity to communications, security, and student safety."

"Oh," you say. Minetta's a *computer!* "Nice to meet you."

Kid Empire shouts, "Minetta, we're going to play ball!"

Zzzzip! Saratoga appears out of nowhere and says, "We try to catch the ball. Minetta tries to stop us."

You suspect it's not really that simple.

GO ON TO THE NEXT PAGE.

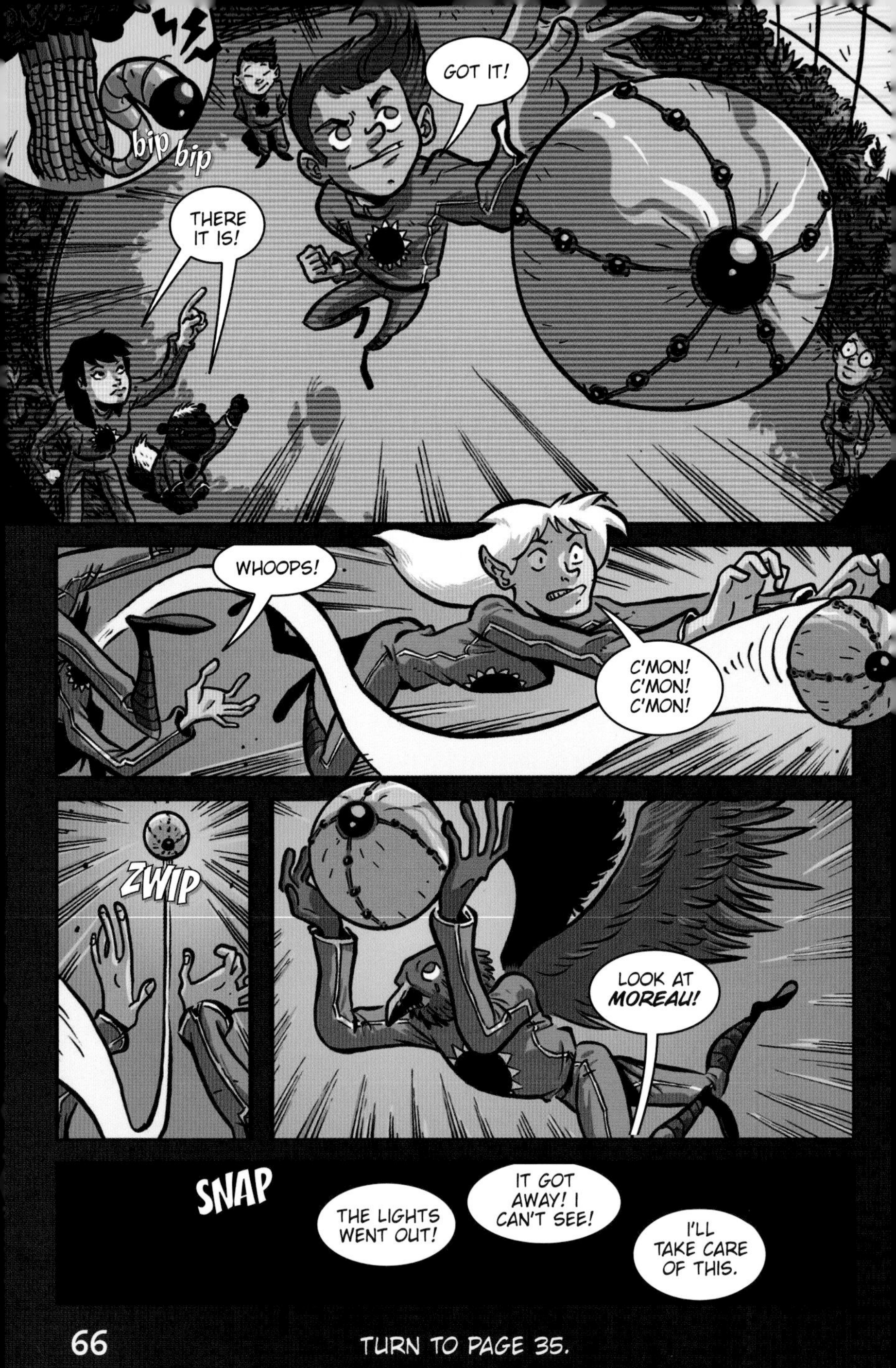
bip bip
GOT IT!
THERE IT IS!
WHOOPS!
C'MON! C'MON! C'MON!
ZWIP
LOOK AT MOREAU!
SNAP
THE LIGHTS WENT OUT!
IT GOT AWAY! I CAN'T SEE!
I'LL TAKE CARE OF THIS.

TURN TO PAGE 35.

You say, "We can't wait for help! It's our turn to protect people!"

Saratoga shouts, "Yeah, let's go!" She runs so fast that she's just a blur over the water. Kid Empire grows to giant size and wades into the harbor. Hayden tells you to get on her back and she flies up. Other students also take off flying in a ragtag band heading for Gowanus.

Gowanus has moved north and onto shore by the time you catch up to him. Although he's getting hit with fire, water, and even energy bolts from Hayden, he's just too big. You and the rest of the students slow him down only a little bit. You need to stop him fast before he destroys the city.

You look around and realize you're near Central Park. On many weekends, your parents have taken you to the park and its museums.

You have an idea! You tell Hayden to fly you to the Natural History museum.

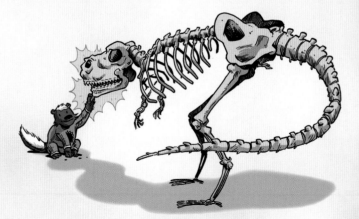

GO ON TO THE NEXT PAGE.

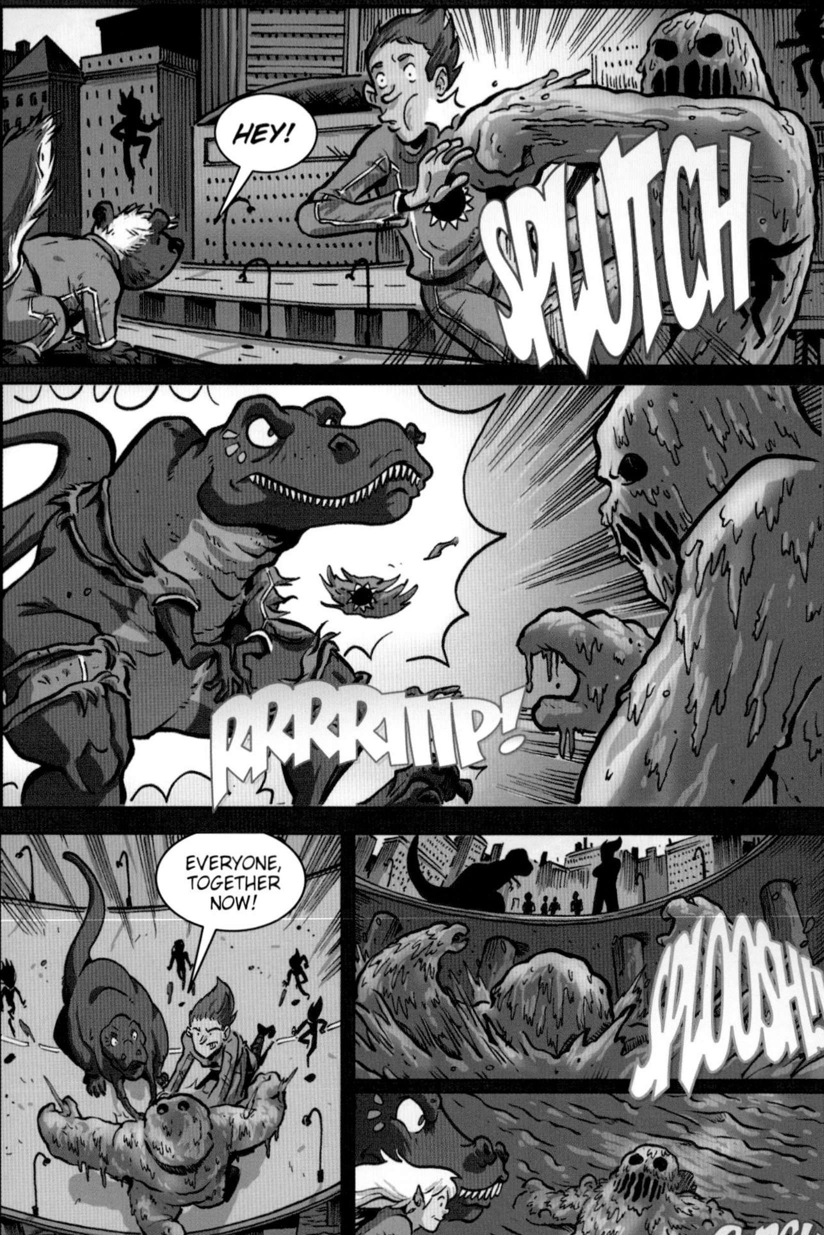
HEY!
SPLUTCH
RRRRRIIIP!
EVERYONE, TOGETHER NOW!
SPLOOSH!!
GURGLE
I THINK WE ACTUALLY DID IT!

GO ON TO THE NEXT PAGE.

"Yes, you did," says a voice. You all turn around in surprise to see the Blue Squad.

One of the Blue Squad members says, "Looks like we weren't needed after all," and you realize it's Miss Starling. The Ellis Academy teachers *are* the Blue Squad!

They escort the students safely back to school. A much smaller Gowanus is taken to Hart Island Prison, bitterly complaining about meddling kids.

Dr. Ellis, the head of the academy *and* the Blue Squad, lectures the students about reckless behavior, but it's obvious that the teachers are very proud of all of you. After this adventure, everyone works hard to learn how to fight as a team. You, Hayden, Kid Empire, and Saratoga become best friends over the years.

The proudest day of your life comes when Miss Starling and Dr. Ellis welcome you and your friends as members of the Blue Squad. You've joined your heroes at last!

THE END

Greenwich looks as if he's about to attack you, so you say, "I'll help you."

Colonel Plum gloats. "We'll grind the world beneath our heels!"

You have to wait for the right moment. Greenwich is keeping an eye on you.

You edge closer to the gate. The lights all turn green, and the space inside the gate goes dark. It's about to open!

You have to take a chance on what Colonel Plum told you about being a singularity. Plants shoot out from Greenwich's arms, but they only brush against your back as you leap through the gate.

There's a bright flash as the machine explodes to pieces around you . . . and you pass out!

You wake up in a cold, barren world. The sky's a strange color, and the air is bitter. You stagger to your feet, hoping to find a way back to the home you just saved.

THE END

TWISTED JOURNEYS®

This is the choice you've been searching for.

WILL YOU . . .

. . . jump into the action?
TURN TO PAGE 4.

. . . look for adventure elsewhere?
TURN TO PAGE 112.

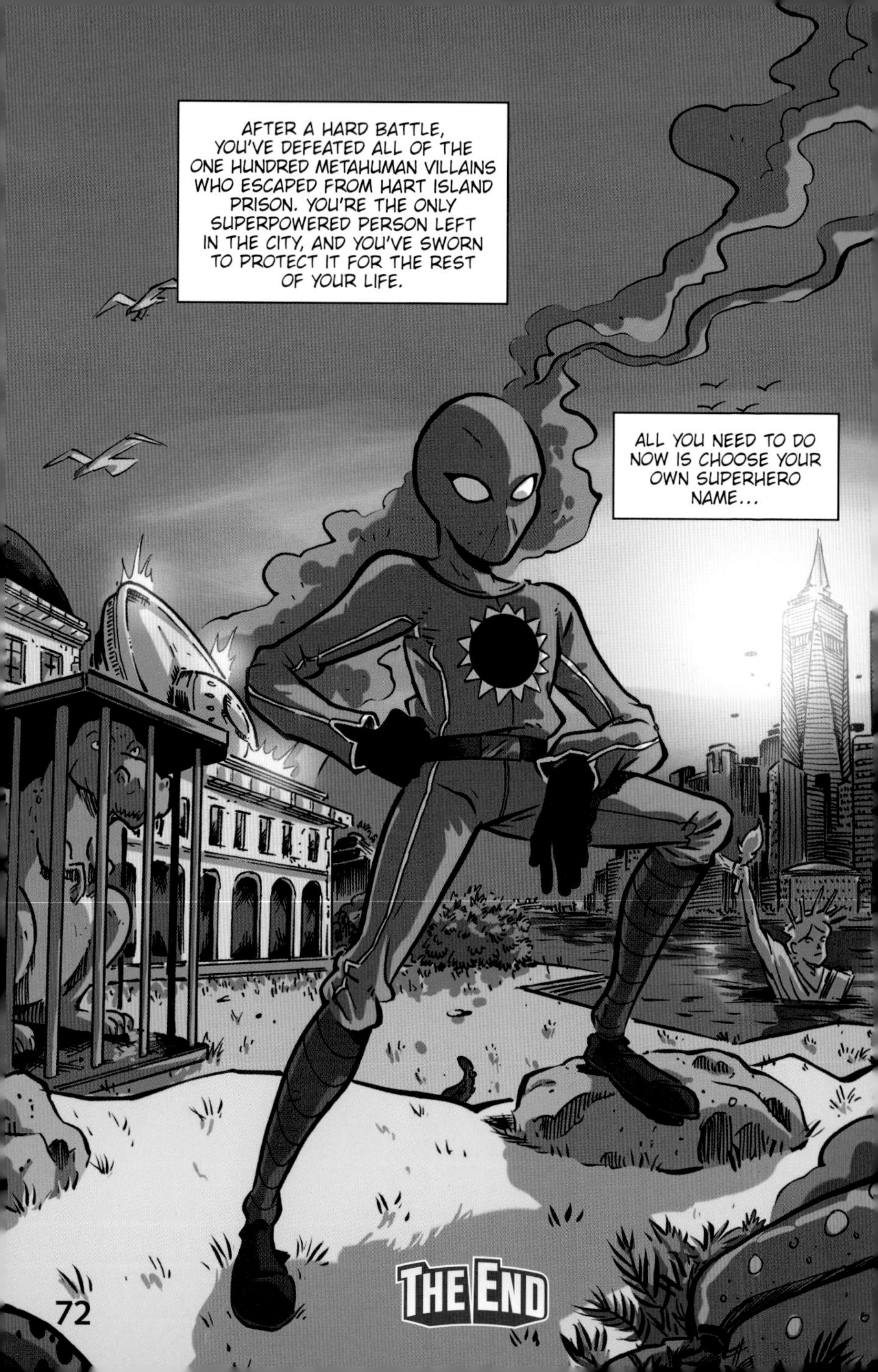
AFTER A HARD BATTLE, YOU'VE DEFEATED ALL OF THE ONE HUNDRED METAHUMAN VILLAINS WHO ESCAPED FROM HART ISLAND PRISON. YOU'RE THE ONLY SUPERPOWERED PERSON LEFT IN THE CITY, AND YOU'VE SWORN TO PROTECT IT FOR THE REST OF YOUR LIFE.
ALL YOU NEED TO DO NOW IS CHOOSE YOUR OWN SUPERHERO NAME...
THE END

"I play a lot of sports," you tell Nightdragon. "I do well in gymnastics."

The Dragonmobile speeds quickly through New York City. You can barely make out the landmarks as you whiz by. The inside of the Dragonmobile is all blinking lights and shiny dials. You're sorely tempted to touch the dashboard controls, but you know better.

"Those are excellent skills," Nightdragon says. "You're acrobatic and have good spatial reasoning skills."

"Well, I'm not a trapeze artist or anything, but, yeah, I can jump long and high, and I can judge distances pretty well. Why is that important?"

"It means you can come with me on patrol and find your parents. You will be my Bluebird."

That's amazing! Nightdragon—*the* Nightdragon—is asking you to be his crime-fighting partner!

GO ON TO THE NEXT PAGE.

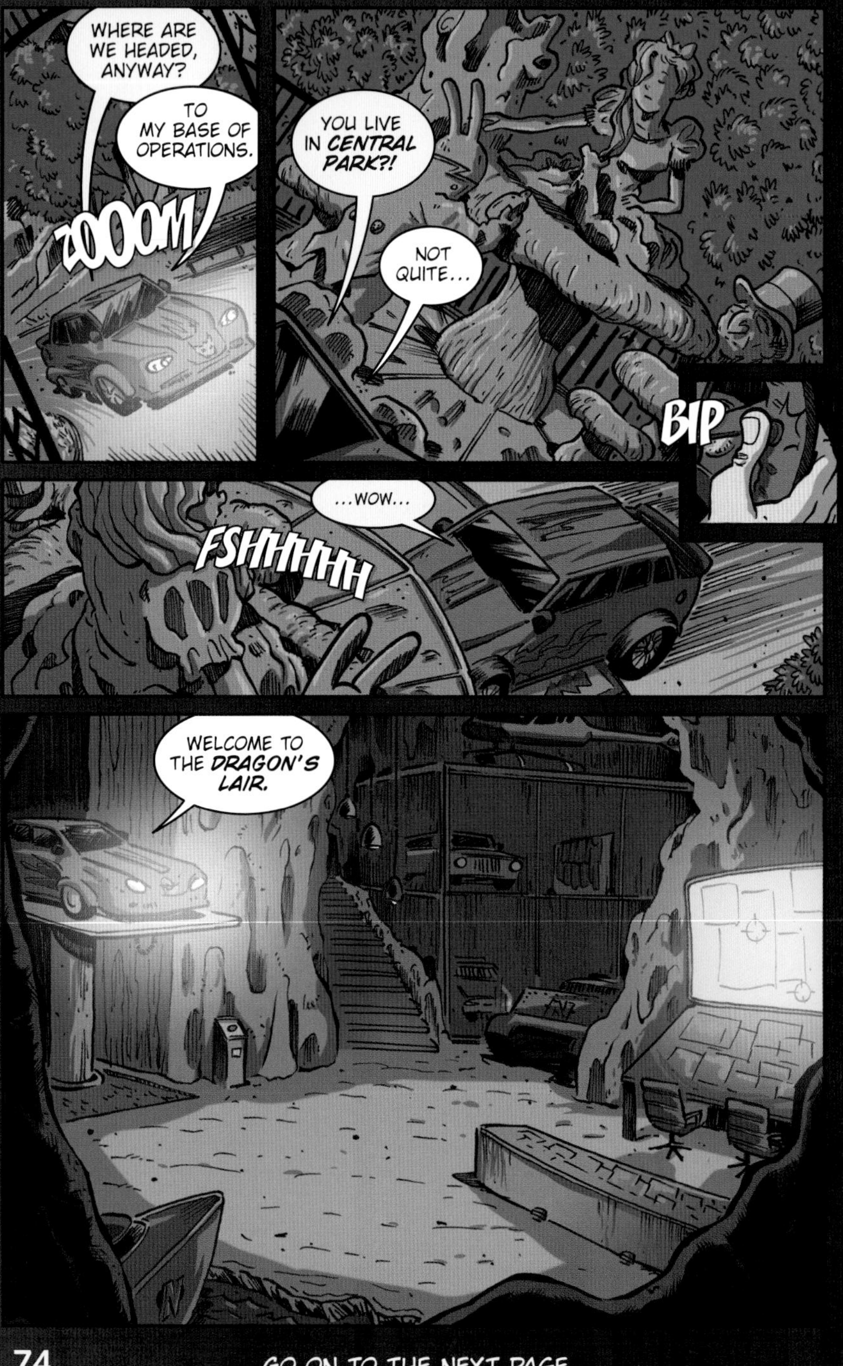
WHERE ARE WE HEADED, ANYWAY?
TO MY BASE OF OPERATIONS.
ZOOOM
YOU LIVE IN CENTRAL PARK?!
NOT QUITE...
BIP
...WOW...
FSHHHHHH
WELCOME TO THE DRAGON'S LAIR.

GO ON TO THE NEXT PAGE.

You don't know where to look first!

"Why do you have a tractor?" you ask.

"It's from one of my earlier adventures," Nightdragon replies. "I thought I would use it more often. Needless to say, the Dragon-Combine was not a sound investment. The Dragonwing, the Dragonfly, and the Dragonboat, however, are quite useful."

You step out of the Dragonmobile. Nightdragon goes to his large computer bank and starts typing. When he finishes, a costume pops out of one side of the machinery.

"Put this on," Nightdragon says. You do so, and Nightdragon declares, "You are now officially Bluebird, my partner, my comrade, my chum."

As you admire your new costume, you see glass cases around the lair filled with strange objects, such as a popsicle that isn't melting even in the warm cavern and a stack of fake bills. It's like a weird museum display.

GO ON TO THE NEXT PAGE.

Which item piques your curiosity the most?

WILL YOU
ASK ABOUT . . .

. . . the popsicle that won't melt?
TURN TO PAGE 58.

. . . the stack of counterfeit money?
TURN TO PAGE 41.

"We have no idea what's out there," you say.

Your dad says, "The only thing we do know is that Tweed is the boss here. So let's go find him."

Outvoted, your mom reluctantly agrees. When you try ramming your shoulder into the door, it falls into the hallway with a loud clang. "Wow. You're superstrong, kiddo," says Dad.

You can hear guards coming! Together you run in the opposite direction, taking random turns to get farther away. You end up in a corridor lined with wide, padlocked doors that smells like a zoo. The noise of the crowd is pretty loud, so you must be near the actual fighting arena.

Suddenly, you see the shadows of guards coming. You retreat deeper into the corridor. But it's a dead end!

Your parents take turns burning and freezing the padlock on one of the doors to weaken and break it. You fling the door open.

Too bad the room on the other side is already occupied . . .

THE END

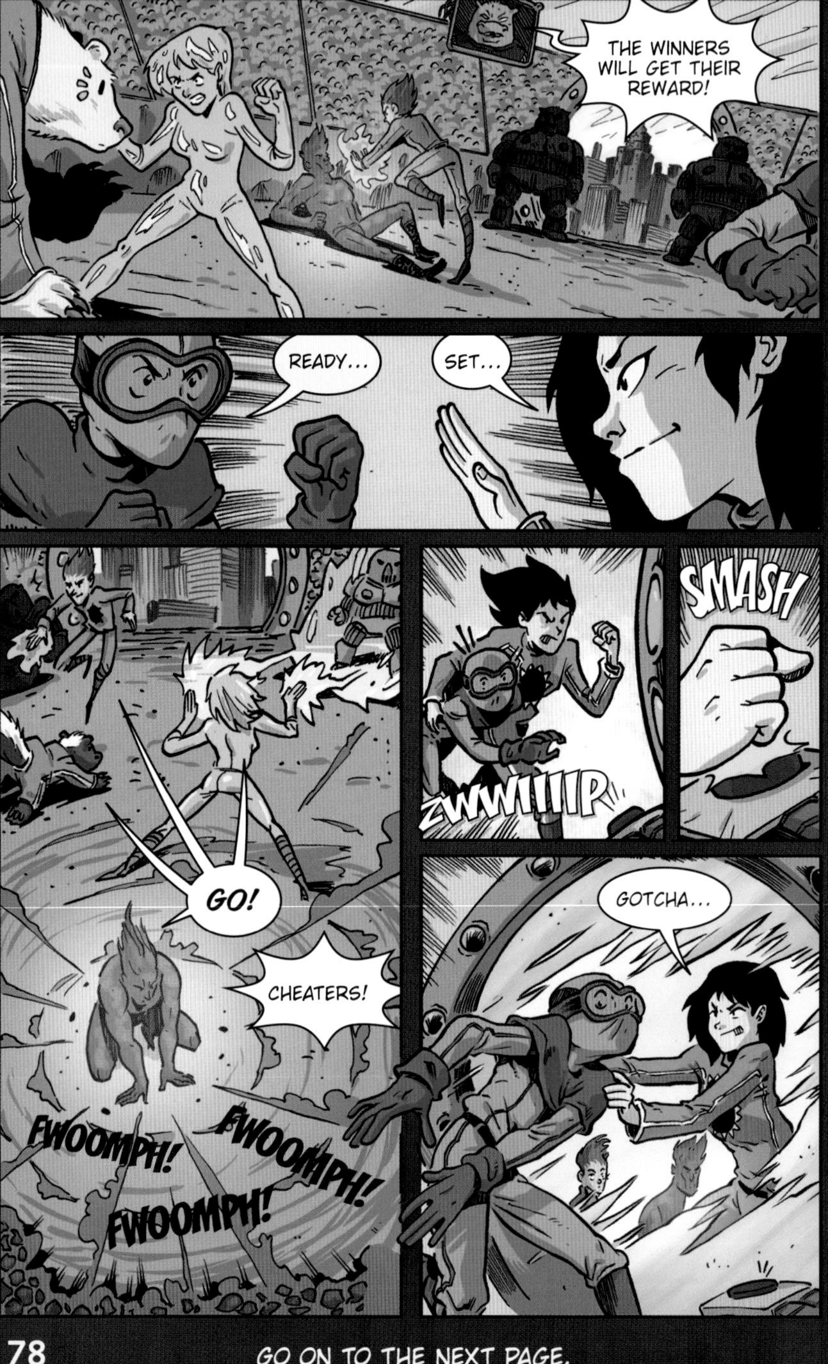
THE WINNERS WILL GET THEIR REWARD!
READY...
SET...
GO!
SMASH
ZWWIIIIP
CHEATERS!
GOTCHA...
FWOOMPH!
FWOOMPH!
FWOOMPH!

GO ON TO THE NEXT PAGE.

With a loud *whoosh,* the gate closes behind you. You watch nervously, but it stays closed. Hopefully forever.

You are safely back home. But home will never be the same—you all have superpowers now.

You take a pledge to join together as a new super-team. Together you stand ready to protect planet Earth from Tweed and all the other villains who threaten our world.

THE END

Nightdragon switches on a viewscreen, pinpointing a location. Using the controls on the dashboard, you zoom in on the area called the Upper East Side, then get the screen to show the businesses on the map. The map is pointing to a place called The Knot.

You've heard that name on the news. "Isn't that the nightclub owned by Oswin Cooper?"

"Otherwise known as the supercriminal gangster the Osprey," Nightdragon says. "He's in the know about all underhanded activity in the city. So he might know who took your parents. And stop touching things."

"I'm sorry." You're ashamed you didn't ask for permission. "But I'm really good with computers."

Nightdragon raises an eyebrow. "Kid, you might be even more useful than I thought. You're my new Bluebird, at least until we find your parents."

"Didn't the last Bluebird get eaten by a sludge monster?" you ask.

Nightdragon sets his jaw. "I failed the first Bluebird. That will never happen again."

"I believe you," you say. "And I'm honored to be your partner."

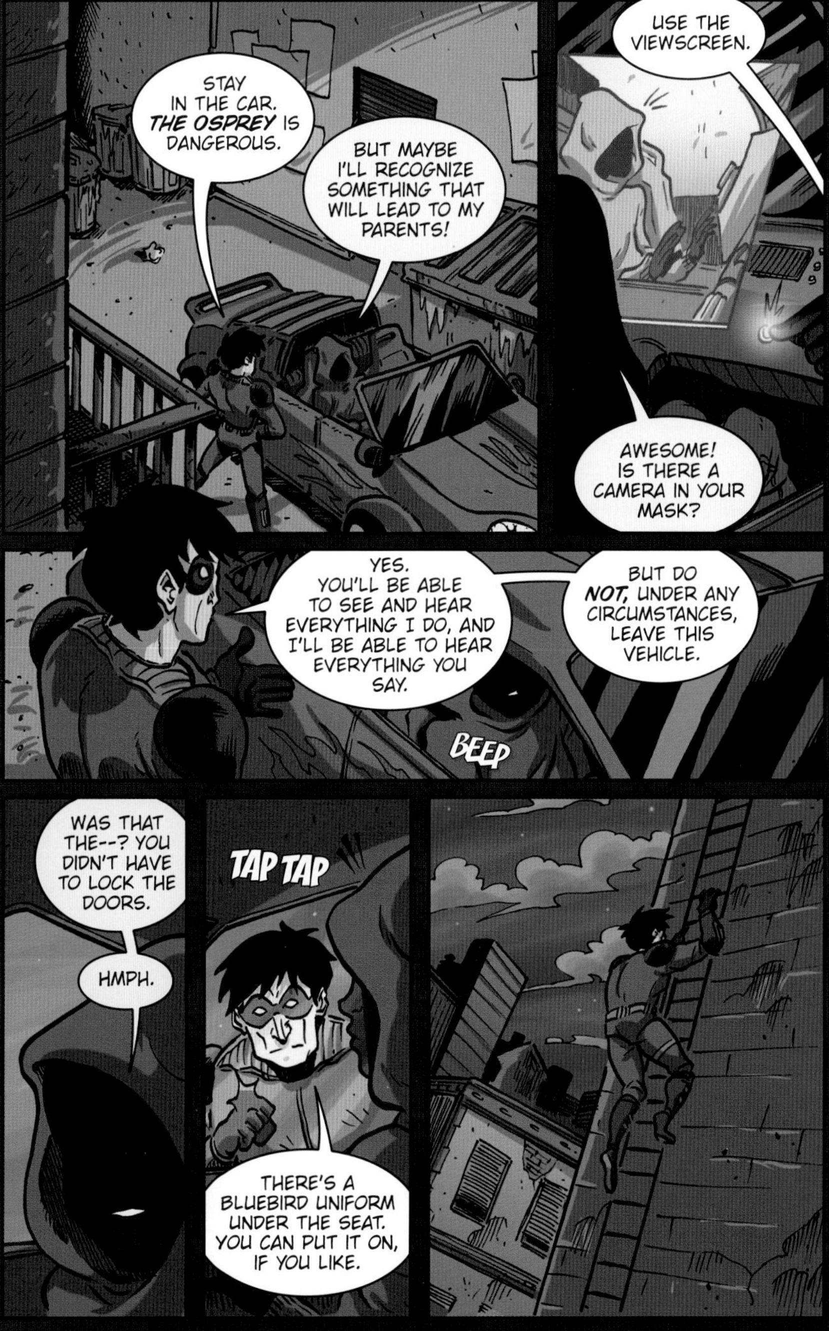
STAY IN THE CAR. THE OSPREY IS DANGEROUS.
BUT MAYBE I'LL RECOGNIZE SOMETHING THAT WILL LEAD TO MY PARENTS!
USE THE VIEWSCREEN.
AWESOME! IS THERE A CAMERA IN YOUR MASK?
YES. YOU'LL BE ABLE TO SEE AND HEAR EVERYTHING I DO, AND I'LL BE ABLE TO HEAR EVERYTHING YOU SAY.
BUT DO NOT, UNDER ANY CIRCUMSTANCES, LEAVE THIS VEHICLE.
BEEP
WAS THAT THE--? YOU DIDN'T HAVE TO LOCK THE DOORS.
HMPH.
TAP TAP
THERE'S A BLUEBIRD UNIFORM UNDER THE SEAT. YOU CAN PUT IT ON, IF YOU LIKE.

TURN TO PAGE 63.

You go upstairs with Greenwich. He tells you to gather the students into a room that he'll fill with sleeping gas.

When Greenwich goes to prepare the room, you run to warn the others. Everyone scatters into hiding places. It's a long, scary day as the alien army hunts for the students.

The teachers eventually return and drive the army back through the gate. You're so tired that you aren't even excited when you find out that your teachers are the secret superhero team called the Blue Squad.

Academy life goes back to normal, but your powers grow weaker as you get older. You can still see enough of the future to give good advice. When you graduate, you become the academy's guidance counselor. You advise students on using their powers for good and even give advice when one of them starts dating a monster.

You never find a way to rescue the kid who was taken through the gate. No matter how much good you do in life, you're haunted by that memory . . . and by how close you came to choosing darkness instead of heroism.

THE END

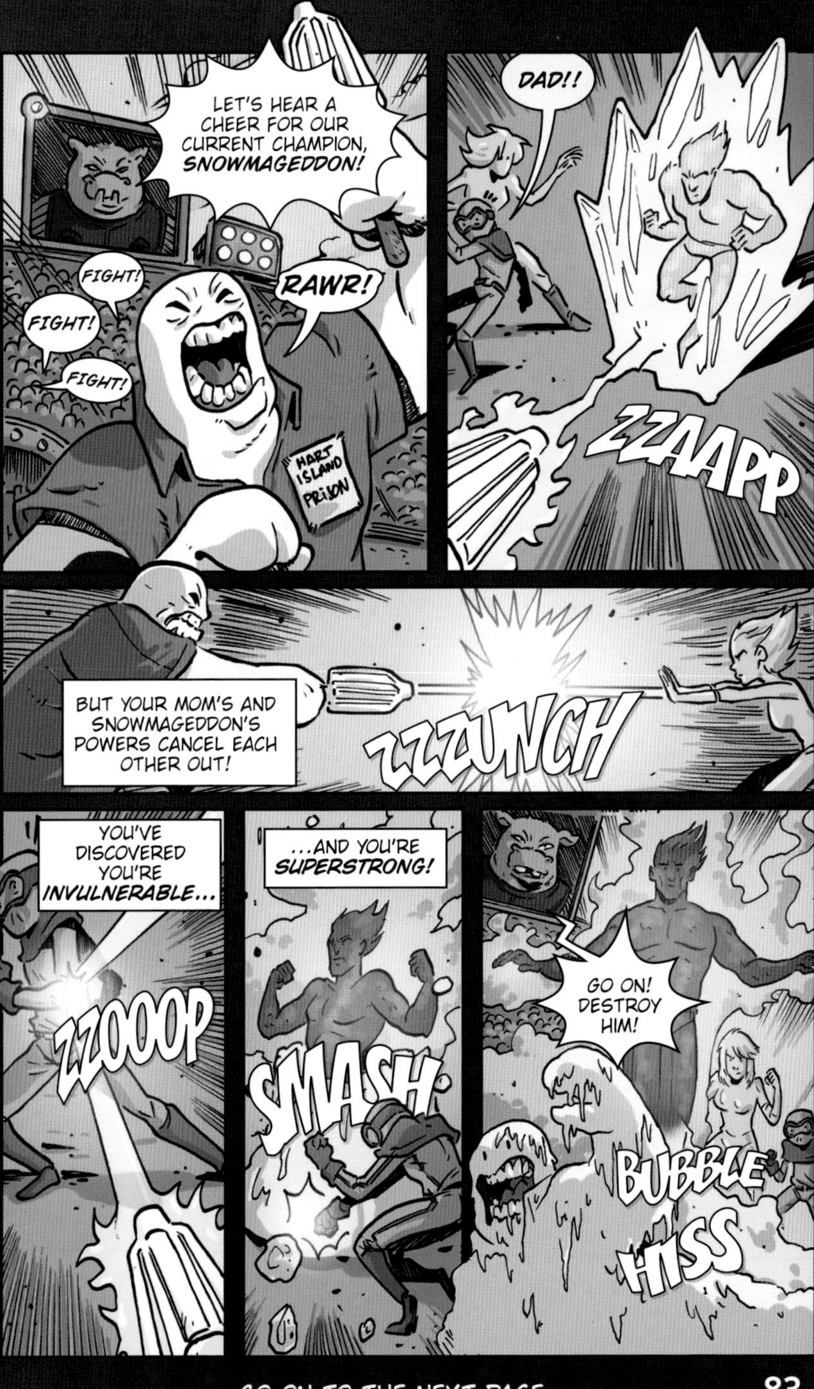
LET'S HEAR A CHEER FOR OUR CURRENT CHAMPION, SNOWMAGEDDON!
FIGHT!
FIGHT!
FIGHT!
RAWR!
HART ISLAND PRISON
DAD!!
ZZAAPP
BUT YOUR MOM'S AND SNOWMAGEDDON'S POWERS CANCEL EACH OTHER OUT!
ZZZUNCH
YOU'VE DISCOVERED YOU'RE INVULNERABLE...
ZZOOOP
...AND YOU'RE SUPERSTRONG!
SMASH
GO ON! DESTROY HIM!
BUBBLE
HISS

GO ON TO THE NEXT PAGE.

TWISTED JOURNEYS®

If you give in to Tweed's demand,
he may let you go.

WILL YOUR FAMILY . . .

. . . refuse to keep fighting?
TURN TO PAGE 22.

. . . destroy the monster while you still have the
strength to win?
TURN TO PAGE 98.

Your parents need help *now,* and you can't wait for Nightdragon to get here!

Bluebird barrage! With the element of surprise and a flurry of blows, you quickly take both henchmen down. "Ha!" you shout proudly. "That wasn't so hard."

"Ha ha!"

You turn and see five more henchmen coming out of the darkness behind your parents.

"It was funny watching those two bums get beat up by a kid, but playtime's over now," one of the henchmen says.

You fight valiantly, but there's just too many of them. You drop in a painful heap. The henchmen stand in a ring around you.

"Nightdragon . . ." you whisper. "Help me . . ."

"Kid," a henchmen says, "I don't know what you were thinking, wearing that getup, but you ain't no Nightdragon. And we ain't gonna let you grow up to *be* one."

You hope Nightdragon can save your parents, because your superhero career is now over. Forever.

THE END

You say, "All right, I'm in."

Colonel Plum grins and says, "Wonderful! I knew you'd be a smart one!"

The gate lights all turn green. A deep hum fills the room as the gate turns into a window to another world. Two armored figures wait on the other side.

Colonel Plum says, "The larger fellow is Tweed, the leader of the army. The other one is his advisor. Are they trustworthy?"

You concentrate until you can see the future. "The advisor will betray us," you report. "Get him out of the way, and the army is yours."

Colonel Plum nods and opens the gate. As soon as the two figures step through, Greenwich attacks the advisor.

Tweed leaps out of the way. He watches coldly as his advisor is overwhelmed by Greenwich's tangling vines. "He would have destroyed our plans," explains Colonel Plum quickly. "Now, nothing stands in the way of victory for both of us!"

GO ON TO THE NEXT PAGE.

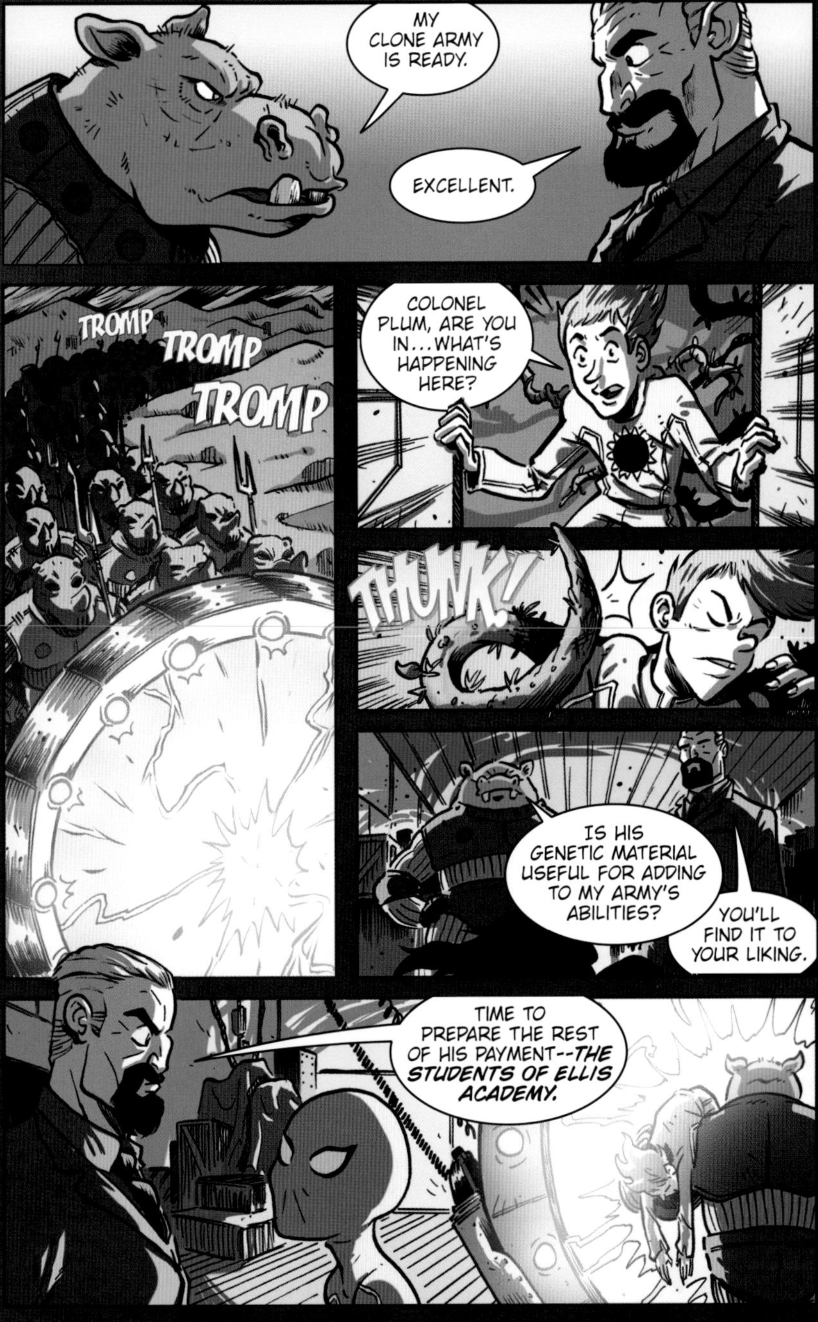
MY CLONE ARMY IS READY.
EXCELLENT.
TROMP
TROMP
TROMP
COLONEL PLUM, ARE YOU IN...WHAT'S HAPPENING HERE?
THUNK!
IS HIS GENETIC MATERIAL USEFUL FOR ADDING TO MY ARMY'S ABILITIES?
YOU'LL FIND IT TO YOUR LIKING.
TIME TO PREPARE THE REST OF HIS PAYMENT--*THE STUDENTS OF ELLIS ACADEMY.*

WILL YOU . . .

. . . keep helping Colonel Plum? Too bad for the other students, but you've already predicted that you'll come out on top!
TURN TO PAGE 37.

. . . warn the students?
TURN TO PAGE 82.

You turn off the television, pick up your backpack, and hurry downstairs. This is one school day you don't want to miss!

You tell your parents, "There was a breakout at Hart Island Prison! They think supervillain master-criminal Amsterdammerung did it!"

Your dad says, "We'll need to keep an eye out on the drive to the boarding school, but we should be OK. Let's load up." He rolls your suitcase out to the car and puts it in the trunk.

Your mom looks a little worried. She hugs you before you walk out to the car together. She says, "Oh, sweetheart, I'm going to miss you so much."

"I'll be home for the holidays," you remind her, and she looks more cheerful.

The highway doesn't have a lot of traffic this early, and it doesn't take long to get into Manhattan.

GO ON TO THE NEXT PAGE.

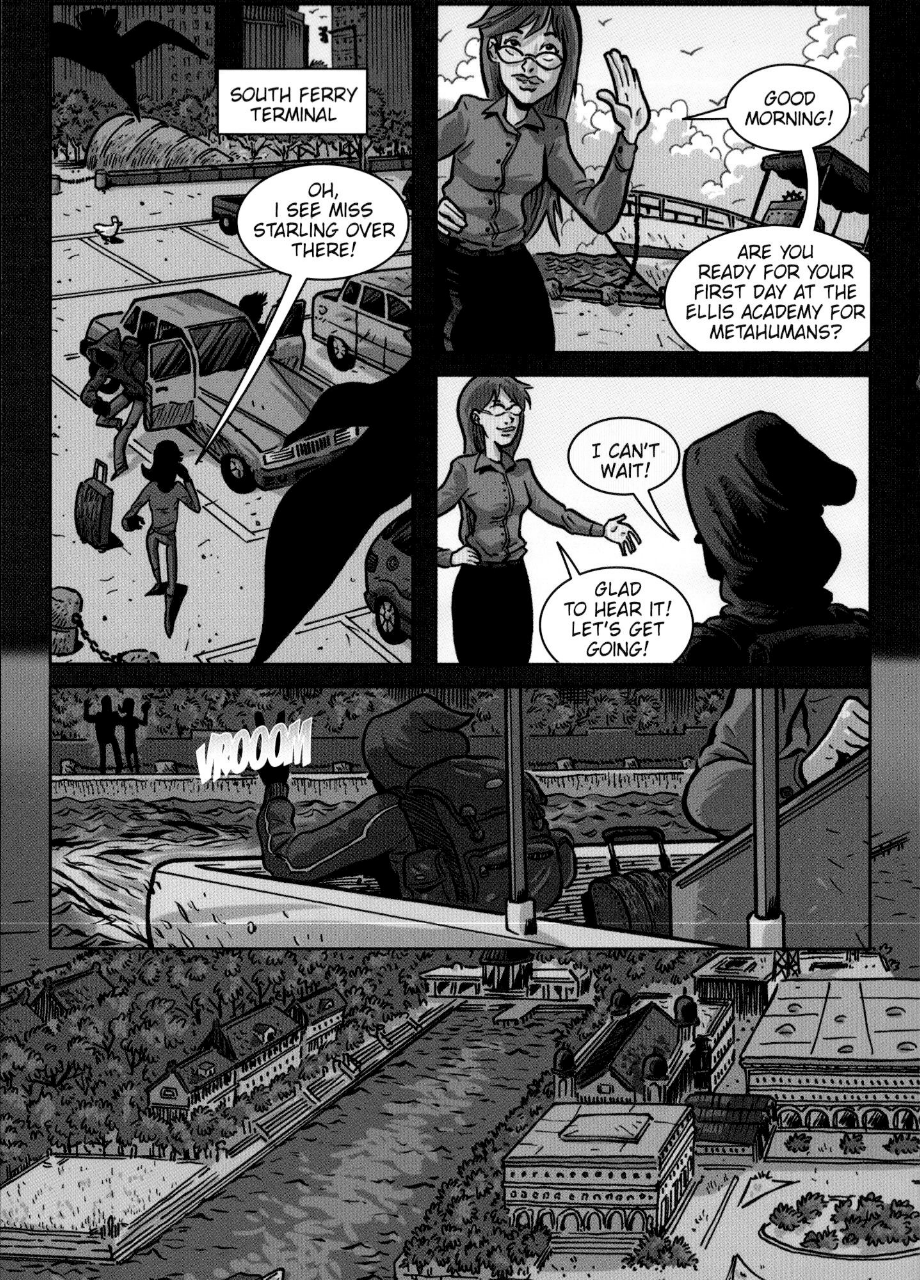
SOUTH FERRY TERMINAL
OH, I SEE MISS STARLING OVER THERE!
GOOD MORNING!
ARE YOU READY FOR YOUR FIRST DAY AT THE ELLIS ACADEMY FOR METAHUMANS?
I CAN'T WAIT!
GLAD TO HEAR IT! LET'S GET GOING!
VROOOM

GO ON TO THE NEXT PAGE.

There's a school uniform waiting for you on the boat. You change into it and already feel like part of the academy. Miss Starling ties the boat up to a small dock and takes you into the Ellis Academy. She says, "Dr. Ellis, the head of the academy, apologizes for not greeting you personally. She has business off the island this morning."

You follow her into a room with windows for walls and filled with plants and flowers. Miss Starling says, "This is the conservatory. And now I have business elsewhere too. Colonel Plum should be here in a moment to show you to your room."

You must look a little lost, because she reassures you, "Your talent is a wonderful gift, and we're going to help you learn to use it. I'm very glad to have you with us."

With that, she hurries out, and you're alone. For about a second. Excited kids pop out from hiding behind plants and quickly surround you.

"Where are you from?"

"What's your superpower?"

GO ON TO THE NEXT PAGE.

These must be your fellow students.

WILL YOU
TELL THEM . . .

. . . you can see the future?

TURN TO PAGE 109.

. . . you're a shapeshifter?

TURN TO PAGE 102.

You climb back up onto the platform and see a large pack of dogs about to attack Erytheia.

"Hey! Over here, doggies!" you shout, stomping your feet.

The whole pack turns toward you, growling. While they're distracted, Erytheia stumbles to her feet. "Bring it on, furballs," you yell at the pack.

The pack rushes at you. You barely manage to sidestep. Several of the dogs slide over the platform edge, yelping. The rest of the dogs twist back toward you and eye you hungrily.

You close your eyes, waiting for the pain of a dozen toothy bites, but instead, you hear a cracking sound. You open your eyes. Erytheia is using her rope like a whip. The dog pack scatters, running away from the sharp blows.

You're about to thank her when you hear Nightdragon shout in pain.

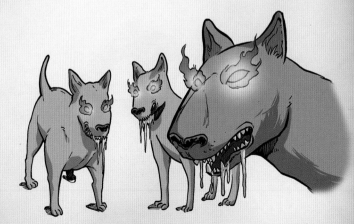

GO ON TO THE NEXT PAGE.

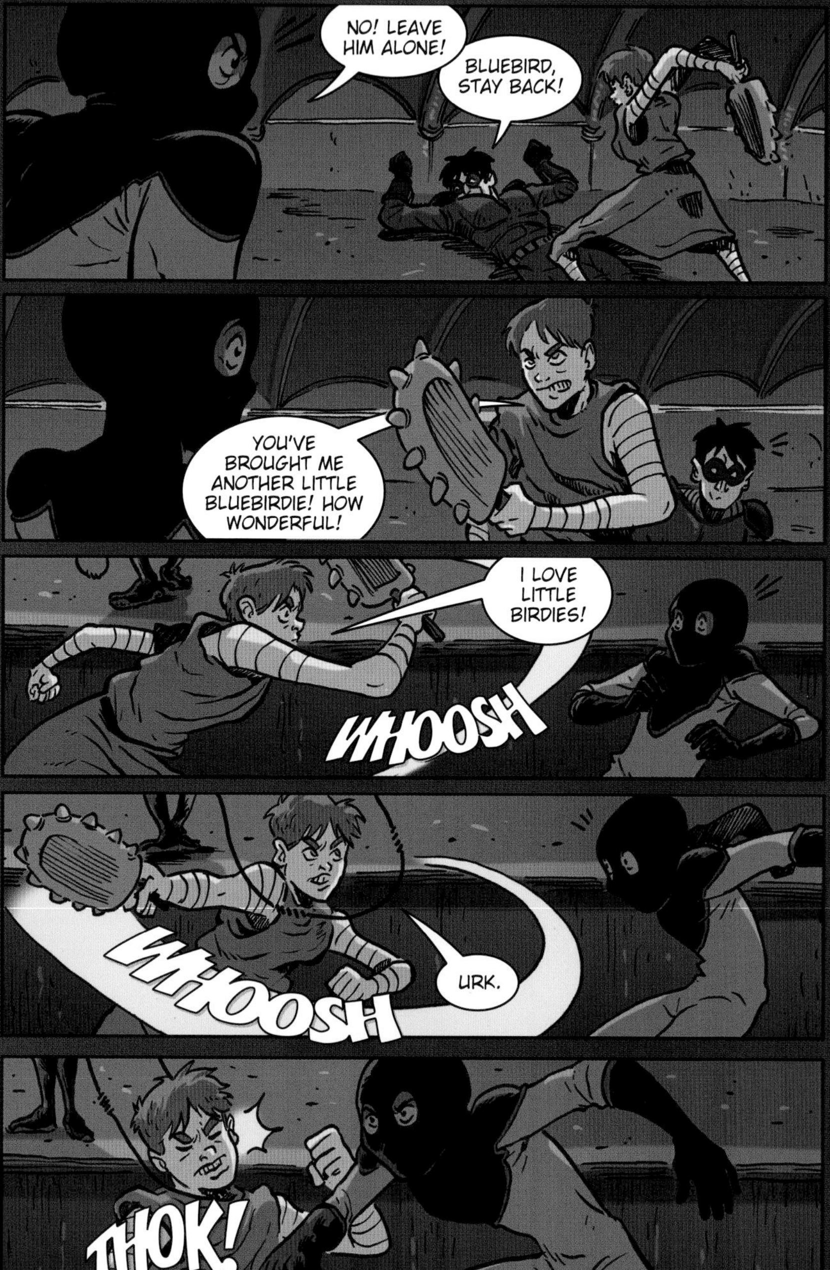
NO! LEAVE HIM ALONE!
BLUEBIRD, STAY BACK!
YOU'VE BROUGHT ME ANOTHER LITTLE BLUEBIRDIE! HOW WONDERFUL!
I LOVE LITTLE BIRDIES!
WHOOSH
WHOOSH
URK.
THOK!

GO ON TO THE NEXT PAGE.

Nightdragon quickly finishes tying up the Terrier while you and Erytheia search for your parents. You find them hidden behind a false wall only moments before the police find you in the abandoned station.

Somehow, Erytheia manages to slip away in the commotion. The police never know she was there. They take the Terrier back into custody. Animal control officers take the dogs away.

You return safely home with your parents. After a while, life returns to normal.

Except for one small detail.

You sneak out almost every night to help Nightdragon fight crime in New York City . . . as the Bluebird.

THE END

Your dad says, "I don't see that we have any choice but to fight."

Tweed grins as he replies, "Well, I like to be polite. Follow the guards to the green room."

Although the walls looked solid, an opening appears. Four guards are standing outside. Each one is huge, and each one has the head of a rhinoceros! Their red armor gleams as they hurry you out of the room. With two guards in front and two behind, you and your family are taken up several levels to a waiting area with couches and platters of little snacks.

The guards lock the door, and you hear them march away. The sound of a roaring crowd comes through the walls.

Your mom says, "I think one of these is an outside wall. We can break through it and get away."

But your dad thinks you should find Tweed. He says, "We could take him hostage and . . . force him to turn us back to normal and free us."

Both plans sound risky without knowing more about this place.

GO ON TO THE NEXT PAGE.

WILL YOU . . .

. . . support your mom and get away from the arena as fast as possible?
TURN TO PAGE 55.

. . . back up your dad and break down the door into the arena?
TURN TO PAGE 77.

With a super punch, you knock out Snowmageddon. Tweed pushes a button. A pit opens up in the arena floor, and Snowmageddon disappears into it.

Every day, Tweed makes you fight a new creature— the Turtle, Osprey, the Mad Terrier. Every day you win the battle. Your next opponent lumbers out to lots of cheers. Tweed announces, "How will the new family of champions do against our favorite fighter . . . *Gowanus?*"

Gowanus is a huge sludge monster. It leaves a trail of steaming mud behind it. It roars at the crowd, then flings a huge blob of stinky slime right at you!

Your mom freezes the blob in midair. You hit it, and it shatters into harmless pieces. The crowd starts booing!

Gowanus throws more slime blobs. You punch aside the ones your mom freezes. Your dad burns the other blobs into nothing. It smells *awful.* The crowd gets angrier and soon they're shouting, "Pit! Pit! Pit!"

You say, "Maybe we'd better knock him out?" But it's too late! The pit opens under your family. Your championship has reached . . .

THE END

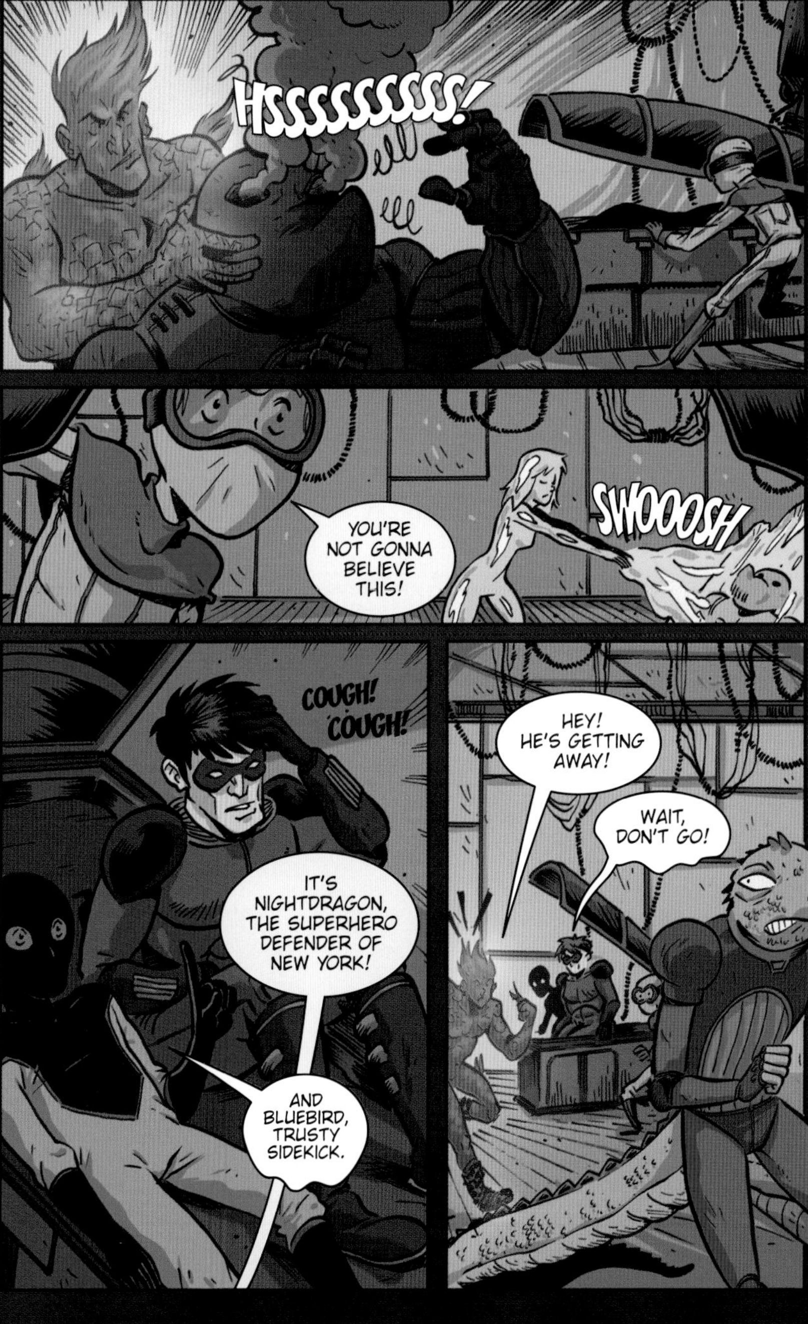
HSSSSSSSSS!
YOU'RE NOT GONNA BELIEVE THIS!
SWOOOSH
COUGH! COUGH!
IT'S NIGHTDRAGON, THE SUPERHERO DEFENDER OF NEW YORK!
AND BLUEBIRD, TRUSTY SIDEKICK.
HEY! HE'S GETTING AWAY!
WAIT, DON'T GO!

GO ON TO THE NEXT PAGE.

That wretched lizard is your best chance
to get home!

WILL YOU . . .

. . . stay with the injured superheroes?
TURN TO PAGE 24.

. . . chase after the lizard man?
TURN TO PAGE 57.

You say, "Maybe it's too much for us to handle."
Hayden gives you a disappointed look, but before she
says anything, Colonel Plum runs up to the group.

He yells, "Everyone get inside! I've contacted the Blue
Squad, and they're on the way."

The students all return to the building and watch
Gowanus from the upper windows. When the battle gets
too far away to see, you keep watching on the news.

Gowanus crawls onto land and destroys several city
blocks before the Blue Squad arrive. You recognize Miss
Starling among the superheroes and realize that the
Ellis Academy teachers *are* the Blue Squad! They drive
Gowanus back into the harbor before defeating him.

You're haunted by the thought that fewer people
would've been hurt if the students had acted. The
teachers reassure everyone that you made
the right choice. However, in your
heart, you vow never
again to stay
back when
the city needs
a hero.

THE END

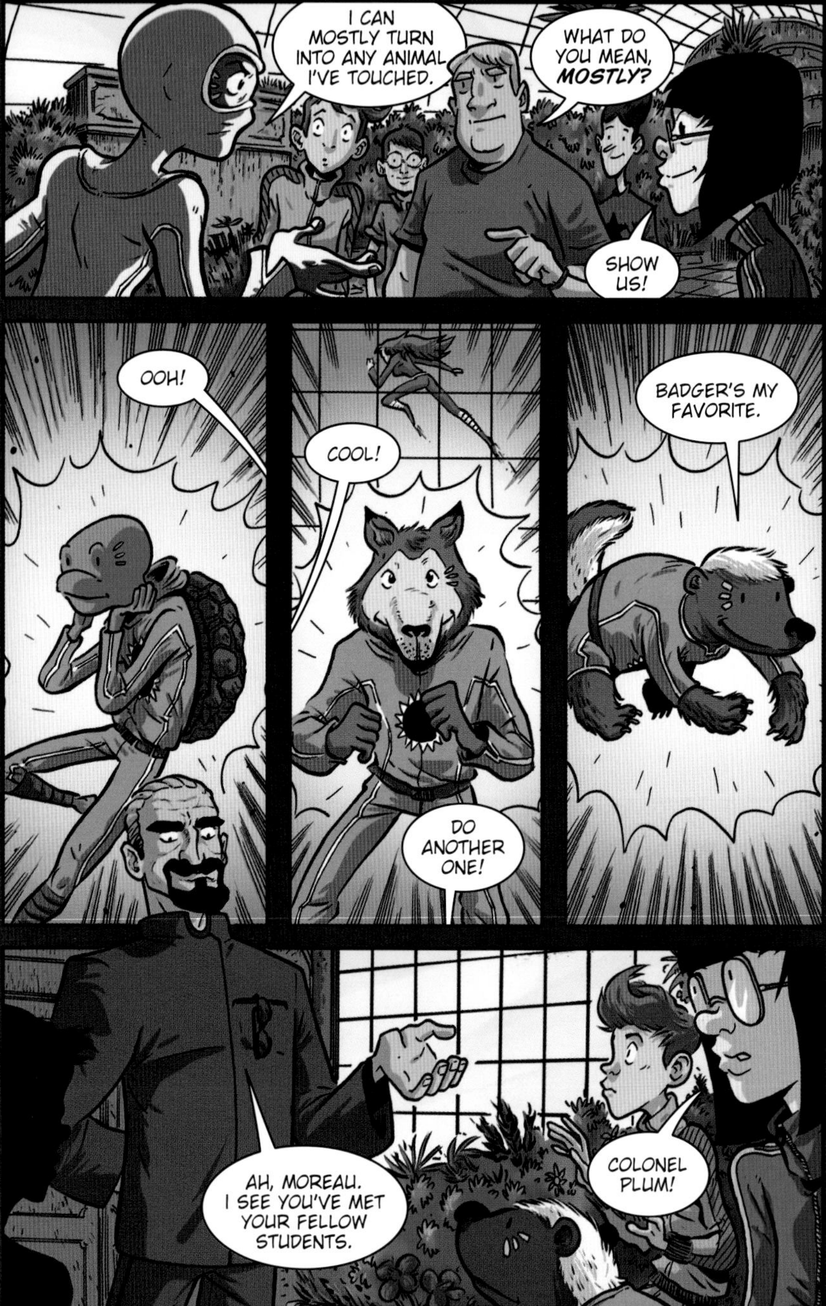
I CAN MOSTLY TURN INTO ANY ANIMAL I'VE TOUCHED.
WHAT DO YOU MEAN, ***MOSTLY?***
SHOW US!
OOH!
COOL!
BADGER'S MY FAVORITE.
DO ANOTHER ONE!
AH, MOREAU. I SEE YOU'VE MET YOUR FELLOW STUDENTS.
COLONEL PLUM!

GO ON TO THE NEXT PAGE.

Colonel Plum raises an eyebrow at the students and says, "Shouldn't you all be getting dressed for class?" With a groan, the other students leave the room.

Colonel Plum grabs your luggage and leads you to your room upstairs on the dormitory level. He says, "It must be a relief to use your powers freely here at the academy. You can finally be yourself."

You're surprised by this. "Won't the whole city see us if we use our powers?" you ask.

"There's a psychic shield protecting the island. No one outside can see what we're doing."

You grin. It sounds great! You've always known that you were adopted and that your parents love you a lot. But they're ordinary humans and they can't help you with your superpowers. You were lucky the Ellis Academy found you last summer, when your superpower kicked in.

GO ON TO THE NEXT PAGE.

"I hope you'll consider me a friend," says Colonel Plum, leaving you alone in the room.

You've just finished unpacking when there's a knock at your door. Three students hurry into your room.

"I thought the colonel would never go!" says a redheaded boy, who introduces himself as Kid Empire. The girl with black hair is called Saratoga, and the girl with white hair is Hayden.

You say, "Colonel Plum seemed OK . . ."

Saratoga makes a face and says, "I don't think Dr. Ellis really wants him around."

"Then why is he here?" you ask.

Kid Empire replies, "It's part of the government deal. He stays, and they let Dr. Ellis use the island for the academy. He's mostly OK."

Saratoga says with a frown, "You haven't seen what—"

Hayden interrupts impatiently. "We came to get Moreau for gym class, remember?"

You're curious about Colonel Plum, but you'd also like to meet the other students.

WILL YOU . . .

. . . ask Saratoga to tell you more?
TURN TO PAGE 12.

. . . go to gym class?
TURN TO PAGE 65.

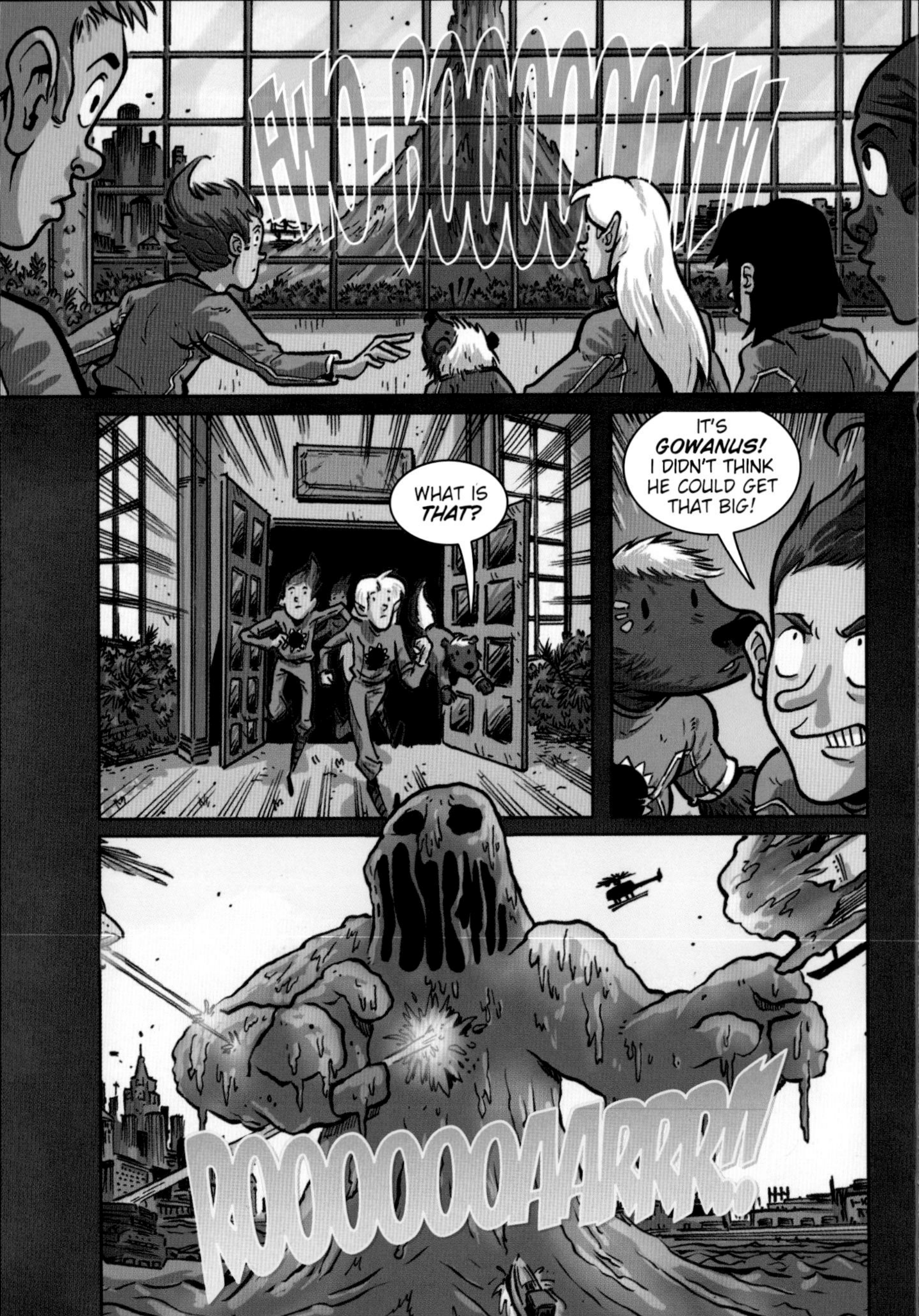
WHAT IS *THAT?*
IT'S ***GOWANUS!*** I DIDN'T THINK HE COULD GET THAT BIG!

GO ON TO THE NEXT PAGE.

Saratoga says, "They won't be able to keep Gowanus from climbing up on land."

Kid Empire grimly agrees, "Yeah, they don't have any metahuman superpowers."

"But all the meta superheroes are dealing with the prison breakout," you say.

You watch Gowanus veer north. It looks as if he'll eventually fight his way around the police force trying to stop him.

"I guess that leaves us," says Hayden.

Everyone stares at one another in shock. You feel a thrill of excitement run through you at the thought of becoming a real hero. But some of the other students look scared.

"We can't fight that thing!"

"Gowanus is too big!"

"The city's in trouble!"

"We should call for help!"

GO ON TO THE NEXT PAGE.

Getting help is definitely the safer thing to do. You're just a bunch of kids. Or maybe it's time for the next generation of heroes to step up.

WILL YOU . . .

. . . rally the others to fight Gowanus?
TURN TO PAGE 67.

. . . call the meta superheroes back to fight?
TURN TO PAGE 101.

You explain that there are many parallel universes. Some of them are very similar to your own reality, with only slight differences. These are called alternate realities.

In those universes, there are other versions of most people, but maybe with a different job or living in another city. Maybe on an important day, the other version made a decision that led to a very different life.

You say, "But there are *no* other versions of me. I'm the only one. It's called being a *singularity*. Dr. Ellis said that I can learn to bend reality because the choices I make are the only possible actions for me. There's no alternate me that does something else."

Some of the students seem to have spaced out. You find your powers kind of confusing too. Dr. Ellis did say that it would take time to figure them out.

You add, "I can see the future—"

A girl runs in. "The Blue Squad just fought an escaped giant sludge monster over by Central Park!" she yells. "They're showing it on the news!"

GO ON TO THE NEXT PAGE.

All the kids stampede out of the room to go watch, except for a green-haired boy who introduces himself as Greenwich—pronounced "gren-itch." He says, "Sorry, they get way more excited about flashy powers that go boom."

You laugh. You're grateful that he hung around. You introduce yourself too. "I'm Waverly."

"Well, Waverly, why don't I show you to your room?"

Greenwich tells you that Colonel Plum's extremely interested in your ability and is eager to meet you. You'd like to get to know your fellow students better, but no one looks up from the television when you walk past the common room.

Your room is bigger than your bedroom at home. You drop off your bags, then Greenwich takes you down to Colonel Plum's basement lab.

110

TURN TO PAGE 25.

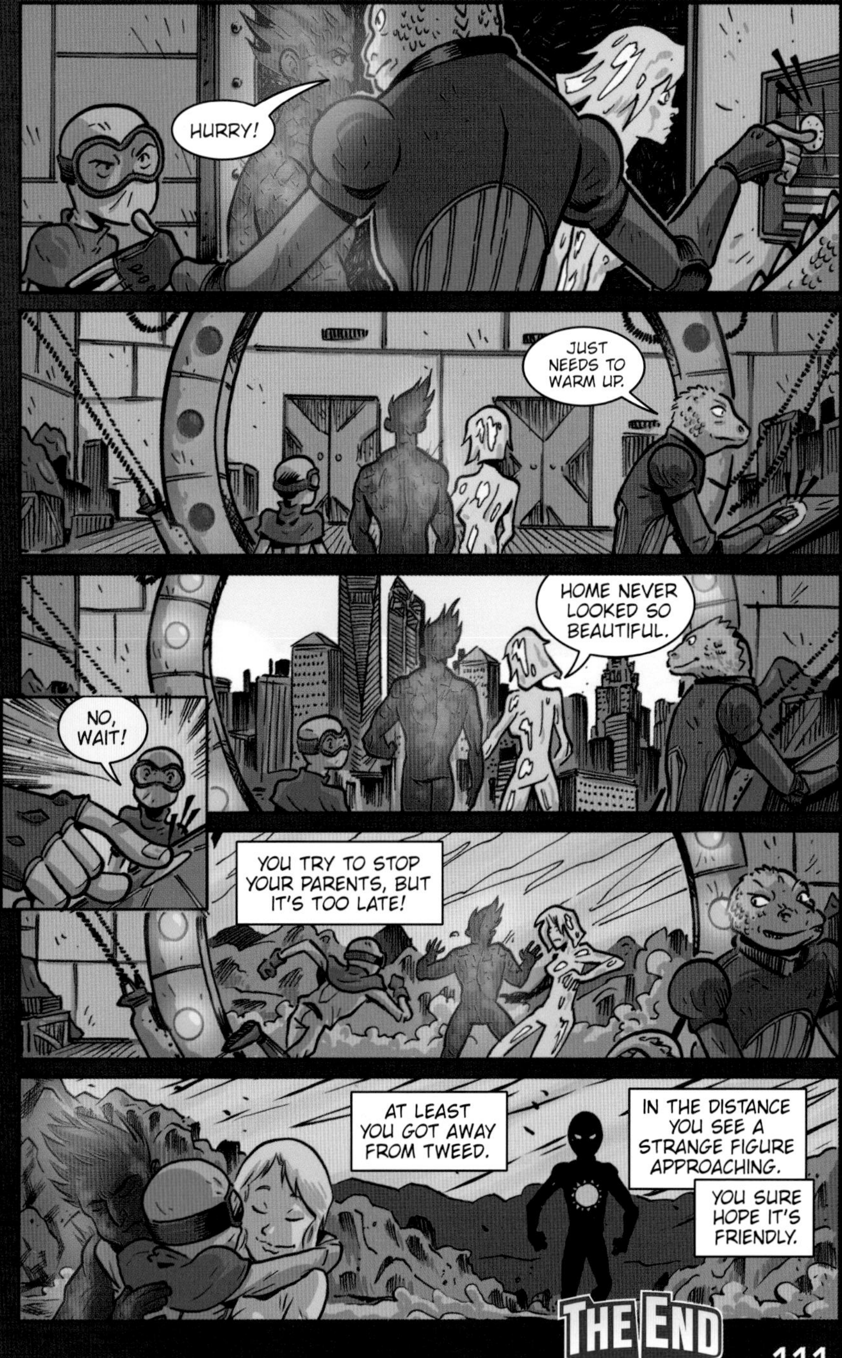

HURRY!
JUST NEEDS TO WARM UP.
HOME NEVER LOOKED SO BEAUTIFUL.
NO, WAIT!
YOU TRY TO STOP YOUR PARENTS, BUT IT'S TOO LATE!
AT LEAST YOU GOT AWAY FROM TWEED.
IN THE DISTANCE YOU SEE A STRANGE FIGURE APPROACHING.
YOU SURE HOPE IT'S FRIENDLY.
THE END

WHICH

TWISTED JOURNEYS®

WILL YOU TRY NEXT?